A SEAL's Strength

A SEAL's Strength

JM Stewart

FOREVER
YOURS

New York   Boston

Copyright © 2017 by JM Stewart
Excerpt from *A SEAL's Honor* copyright © 2017 by JM Stewart
Cover design by Brian Lemus
Cover copyright © 2017 by Hachette Book Group, Inc.

Forever Yours
Hachette Book Group
1290 Avenue of the Americas
New York, NY 10104
forever-romance.com
twitter.com/foreverromance

First ebook and print on demand edition: October 2017

Forever Yours is an imprint of Grand Central Publishing. The Forever Yours name and logo are trademarks of Hachette Book Group, Inc.

The publisher is not responsible for websites (or their content) that are not owned by the publisher.

The Hachette Speakers Bureau provides a wide range of authors for speaking events. To find out more, go to www.hachettespeakersbureau.com or call (866) 376-6591.

ISBN 978-1-5387-2885-7 (print on demand edition)
ISBN 978-1-5387-1176-7 (ebook edition)

A SEAL's Strength

CHAPTER ONE

Gabriel Donovan frowned at his reflection in the full-length mirror, then glanced down at his ten-year-old daughter, Charlotte. She stood in front of him, her gaze intent on her task of knotting his tie. "Why the hell am I doing this again?"

Char frowned her disapproval and darted a glance at him. "You owe the swear jar a dollar, Dad. And you're doing this because you need a date. It's time."

With a heavy sigh, he stuffed a hand in his right front pocket, pulled out a dollar bill and held it out to her. The jar was full already, and the money in there was all his. Some example he was setting.

Char stuffed the bill into her pocket and resumed her task. He turned back to his reflection, frowning at the dress shirt and tie she'd insisted he wear. At least he'd won the jeans argument.

He let his shoulders slump. The whole evening set out before him exhausted him, and it hadn't even started. "I am so not cut out for this. I miss your mother."

Life with Julia had been simple. Reliable. She'd been a constant. He'd been cocky enough back in college to think he was good with women, but he hadn't dated in...hell, before Char was born. He was so far out of practice he might as well be a gangly, uncertain teenager all over again.

Char looped one end of the tie over the other and tipped her head back to look up at him. "I miss her, too, Dad, but you promised you wouldn't be sad forever."

While her face remained stoic, her scowl set firm, he didn't miss the worry and sadness that crept into her eyes. Julia's death had been hard on them both but on Char most of all. His baby sister, Molly, had told him a little girl needed her mother. That she might be right was another reason why he was going on this date. They both could use a change.

He cupped Char's chin in his palm. She looked like a younger version of Julia. The same auburn hair, a shade darker than her mother's. The same oval face and cute, upturned nose. All she'd gotten from him were her hazel eyes and unruly curls. Still, every time he saw her, his chest ached. He wasn't ready to start dating again. Marriage and family had suited him fine. "You're too old for your own good, you know that? You shouldn't be taking care of me. You should just be a kid."

Char was smart like her mother, too. She got straight As in school with little effort, constantly had her nose in a book, and since Julia's death, seemed to have made it her mission to take care of him. It's what they'd done since Julia got sick, how they'd gotten by: they took care of each other. Her enthusiasm for his dating again came from a more basic need, though. She wanted him to stop being sad.

At least, that's what she'd said last week when he'd finally given in and agreed to his sister's cockamamie scheme. The problem was, he wasn't sure *how* to stop being sad. How do you stop missing someone when you'd give both arms to have them back? He also worried about Char. She was positive now, but if it came down to it, would she really accept a new woman's place in his life?

The heavy emotion in Char's eyes lightened, and she shot him a mischievous smile. That was something else she's gotten from him—her playful nature. "Somebody has to take care of you. We'd eat out every night if I didn't make you cook."

A twinge of guilt tightened his stomach. She was right, of course. He couldn't cook to save his life. Julia had always taken care of that. Along with a host of other things, like laundry and grocery shopping. After his parents' deaths, Molly had taken care of what he'd always considered the "girl stuff." Hell, even in the military someone else had always done the cooking. He hated the grocery store. It was too damn crowded and too damn bright. If you asked him, the drive-through was just easier all around.

"I don't know what you have against takeout. Most kids your age could live on the stuff." Gabe turned back to his reflection and poked a finger into his collar. "Is the tie really necessary?"

He hadn't worn one since Julia's funeral. Spending most of his day at the custom motorcycle and repair shop he co-owned with Marcus Denali, a fellow SEAL he'd served with, he had his hands in engine grease the majority of the day. Anything more than a T-shirt would only end up grimy anyway.

Char slipped one end of the tie into the loop she'd made. "Yes. It's nice. Plus, it's blue. That's what they said, right? You have to wear blue so she'll know it's you?"

He sighed and stared at his reflection. For the first time since Julia died three years ago, he had a freakin' date, from a dating service, no less. The wife of one of his mechanics owned the exclusive matchmaking company Military Match. Trent Lawson, also a SEAL and the guy who did most of his custom detailing, had used the place with good results. He and his fiancée, Lauren, were getting married in three months.

"Besides, I like this tie. Mom gave it to you for Christmas before she died. It'll be good luck." Char readjusted his tie and patted his chest, then stood back to eye her handiwork. A self-pleased smile etched across her face. "There. You look perfect."

He shook his head. "I must be out of my mind."

He pinched the bridge of his nose and squeezed his eyes shut for a moment. Three years alone, and he still wasn't ready for this. Though he *was* lonely. He missed the simple things, like not having to sleep alone and waking to warm, soft curves. He also wanted—needed—to finally move beyond the pain and monotony his life had become since Julia's death. He wanted to actually live...not just go through the motions. If only because she couldn't.

What he hoped for tonight he hadn't a clue. Companionship? To get laid? Someone else to talk to besides Char and Molly and the guys at the shop? Hell. He'd figure out the rest when he got there. At the very least, it would get Molly and Char off his case.

The doorbell sounded through the house, and Char's brows shot up, her eyes widening with excitement.

"That's Aunt Molly!" She darted out of the room, her feet thumping down the hall.

Gabe turned from the full-length floor mirror to the picture on the dresser beside him. He touched the glass, tracing the curve of Julia's forehead with his thumb. She'd been healthy then. Alive and vibrant. Her smile still took his breath away. "Wish me luck, Jules."

He drew a deep breath, trying his damnedest to ignore the nausea swirling in his stomach, and followed Char. Emerging into the front room of the house, he found her in the foyer with Molly. Since Julia's death, Molly had taken to helping him with Char. He was grateful to her on that front, because he was in over his head. He hadn't a clue how to raise a little girl. If it were up to him, Char would be in the shop with him, learning how to take apart an engine. Julia had always insisted little girls needed a feminine role model. Luckily for him, Char adored her aunt Molly and loved getting to play with Molly's three girls.

Molly glanced up as he entered the living room. A slow smiled curled across her face, amusement gleaming in her eyes. "Wow. Look at you. Hot stuff."

He glared at her as he approached the foyer. "Stop."

Molly's smile drooped. She turned to Char and tousled her hair. "Why you don't go pack your stuff for the weekend. Give me a minute with your dad."

Char shot him a sideways scowl. "Cheer him up, Aunt Molly. He'll ruin his date."

With a shake of her head, Char strode for her bedroom.

Once she was out of hearing range, Molly turned worried eyes on him.

Gabe held up a hand, stopping the encouragement he'd heard a dozen times since she'd taken it upon herself to sign him up for this date. "Don't start with the 'this is good for you' crap. I get it. You're both right. It's time. But I don't have to like it."

Molly let out a heavy sigh, then, just as suddenly, flashed an over-bright smile. "At the very least, hope that you'll get laid, then."

His heart stalled, and he darted a panicked glance behind him. Char's soft voice echoed up the hallway as she sang some upbeat boy-band tune. When he was satisfied she hadn't overheard Molly's frank comment, his heart resumed its beat. Gabe turned back to his sister and frowned.

"Jesus, Moll, keep your voice down." He shouldn't be surprised she'd said it, though. That was Molly in a nutshell—bold as brass and doing as she pleased. He couldn't stop his cheeks from blazing all the same. "I don't need advice on getting laid from my sister."

She had the nerve to grin at him. "Apparently, you do, because you're not doing it."

He glared at her. "Moll..."

She laughed and held up her hands. "All right, all right. At the very least, try to have a good time. Don't scowl, and for crying out loud, don't sit there brooding." She cuffed his shoulder and winked at him. "You had a personality once. Try to dig it up, huh?"

He let out a heavy sigh. She was right. More times than he cared to admit, he'd bitten her head off for worrying about him too much. Hell, the guys at the shop had pointed out the same thing, how snappish he'd become. Marcus had teased him about it the other day, when he'd lost his temper with a supplier over parts that hadn't come in on time. *"You need to get laid, man."*

Also why he'd found himself with a date tonight. Because Marcus was right. He hadn't had sex with anyone but his left hand since Julia got sick, nearing on four years now. Hell. His freakin' balls were blue. The thought of warm feminine curves against him made his cock twitch in his jeans. If all he got out of this date was that, he'd consider this whole experience successful.

Char came running back to the door, her backpack stuffed full and slung over her shoulder. She hurled herself against him, wrapping her arms tightly around his waist. "Bye, Daddy. I love you."

He bent to kiss the top of her head. "I love you, too, sweetheart. Make sure you mind Aunt Molly, okay?"

She leaned back, hazel eyes wide and anxious and filled with too much worry. "Promise you'll try to have a good time? Mom made me promise that I wouldn't let you sit around and be sad. So you have to promise."

A thick lump formed in his throat. Slayed. Completely, one hundred percent slayed by a ten-year-old.

He brushed the curls out of her face. "I promise I'll try. Now go."

She hugged him again, then slipped her hand into Molly's.

Molly tossed him a friendly smile. "I'll have her back Sunday morning, as usual."

He hooked his thumbs in his belt loops. "Thanks, Moll.

I really appreciate your help, you know. Next weekend's my turn."

In exchange for her help with Char, he took Molly's three girls every other weekend, so that she and her husband, Leo, could have a little time to themselves.

Warmth bloomed in her eyes, her smile softening. "Thanks." Then she punched his shoulder and pursed her lips. "Now you have to promise me you're at least going to try to like this woman."

He couldn't help the soft laugh that left him. Despite being six years younger, Molly had always had a strong motherly streak. An annoying one.

He opened the front door and nodded at the porch beyond. "Will you guys get out? I'll never get there with you two hanging around nagging me to death."

Molly rolled her eyes, but ushered Char out all the same, calling to him as she made her way to her car, parked at the curb. "I'm going to call you tomorrow morning. You'd better not answer."

He shook his head and closed the door. Alone in the deafening silence, he heaved a sigh. The knots in his gut twisted all over again. This particular dating agency's "thing" was supposedly the initial meeting. They set the time and place, and you simply showed up. All he knew about his date tonight was that she was a blond attorney and she'd also be wearing something blue. Hence the damn tie.

According to Karen, the service's owner and his mechanic Mike's wife, the idea was to make the initial meeting seem more like a chance encounter. Add a little mystery. Trent, however, had told him all it really meant was that he'd have a blind date. Trent had loathed that aspect and had offered the information almost as a warning.

Gabe glanced down at his sneakers and stroked a hand down his thigh. At this point, he wasn't above a blind date for his first-ever venture into the land of dating again. He only hoped she wouldn't mind that he was missing the lower part of his left leg.

* * *

Seated on a hard park bench, looking out over the waters of Lake Washington, Stephanie Mason bounced her knee. Nervous anticipation flooded through her. She glanced down at herself, straightening her jacket. A half hour ago, when Lauren, one of her two best friends, suggested she wear this cobalt-blue halter top, it had seemed perfect. A chance to shed the suits she wore to the law firm every day, sexy without being too revealing. Now she had her doubts. It seemed too tame.

Were she going to a club, she'd have worn something a little more revealing. She wasn't a stranger to the dating scene, knew how to flirt, how to dress to lure a man's attention. But she'd done flings for so long now she'd forgotten how to behave on a real date. Lauren, though, the more sensible one of their trio, had pointed out that showing *her goods* wasn't appropriate for a first date she hoped would lead to more than a one-night stand. The question was, would her date like tame? Or should she have insisted on something sexier?

She hitched up the sleeve of her jacket, glanced at her watch for the third time in ten minutes, and heaved a sigh.

Her first real date in two years and the guy was late. Okay, so only by five minutes, but in her profession punctuality was everything. That he was late told her a lot. Namely, that he thought so little of *her* he couldn't be bothered to show up on time.

So much for the old adage "third time's the charm." This was her third date through Military Match, and it wasn't starting out any better than the others had. The first guy she'd met had been so cheap he'd practically squeaked. They'd gone to a matinee show, and he'd paid for dinner with coupons. Freaking coupons. The second guy had spent the whole night talking about himself.

Figures Lauren would go on one date and meet the love of her life. So far Steph had managed only to find guys who were all wrong for her.

Steph glanced down at her top again. Okay, so maybe she should give Lauren more credit. Steph and Mandy, best friend number two, had dressed Lauren conservatively for her date. Lauren had insisted the outfit was more seductive than she was comfortable with, but really, it was conservative by Steph's standards. After all, the top had shown hardly any cleavage, and Lauren had worn jeans and not the flirty little miniskirt Steph had brought over. And look how her date had turned out. She was marrying Mandy's older brother, Trent, a man she'd known for practically her whole life.

Steph lifted her face to the beautiful sky and stared at the few stars peeking out from between the clouds. She'd known Mandy for two years now, since the day she'd hired the cute brunette to help plan her wedding. When Alec had left her standing at the altar, looking and feeling like an utter fool,

Mandy had been the friend she needed. She'd introduced her to Lauren. The two had been childhood friends. That night Mandy had insisted on a girls' night at home. They'd had so much fun, they'd immediately made it a weekly thing.

If ever she'd had sisters, those two would've been it.

Which was why she'd taken Lauren's wardrobe suggestions. More than anything, she wanted to meet someone special. She wanted what Lauren had found—her forever guy. A man with a soft heart and a tender touch. Someone worth sticking around for a while with, but who'd be okay with letting her take things slowly as she finally found her feet again. Since that day, two years ago now, when Alec had stood her up at the altar, she'd been living a lie, determined never to get hurt like that again.

But the truth was, the endless flings she'd once delighted in had worn thin. Deep down she wasn't a single kind of girl. Watching the men leave at the end of the night and then waking alone every morning only served to make her feel exactly that—alone.

It was time to get back out there. Time to risk putting her heart on the line.

Steph turned to scan the area around her again. Even though it was April in the Pacific Northwest, the night was gorgeous. Not quite sixty, with lovely cool breezes and a clear sky, a few stars peeking out from behind the clouds. They usually didn't see days like this until nearly July. Any other time, she'd have put on her Nikes and gone for a run, simply for an excuse to enjoy the break from the ceaseless rain. Apparently, she wasn't alone in that sentiment. A half dozen or so people littered the area.

Her date could be any one of them. Not that she'd recognize him if she saw him. All the woman from Military Match had told her was that he was "huge," had dark hair, and would be wearing something blue. She was told to meet him by the beach, here at Chism Park.

Restless with the need to move, she surged to her feet and turned in a slow circle. Halfway around, a sight stopped her cold. Some twenty feet or so down the sidewalk, a huge hulk of a man stood doing exactly what she was. Hands stuffed in his pockets, he looked around, as if he were waiting for someone.

The sheer size of him, along with the width of his strong shoulders and the dark hair licking at the collar of his black leather jacket sent her stomach into overdrive. The ache of familiarity flooded her veins, her heart beating as if it were trying to escape her chest.

Gabe.

Of all the people to run into, and tonight of all nights. God, he looked exactly the same as he had the last time she'd seen him. Had it really been eleven years? He stood six foot six inches of intimidating, delicious man. She knew from experience every inch of him was solid and every muscle rippled when he moved. Even now his well-fitting jeans clung to his tight ass and showcased the power in his strong thighs.

His hair curled over his forehead, the ends whipping in the slight breeze. Her fingers itched with remembrance. How many times had she brushed those soft curls out of his eyes?

Back in her undergrad days, those big hands and that muscular body had given her so much pleasure. Of all her lovers over the years, he was the one she couldn't forget. He'd been one of the few to truly rock her world. The energy they'd worked up in each other could easily have powered a small city. Eleven years ago she and Gabe had fallen into a "friends-with-benefits" relationship. They'd hung out, discussing classes and dick professors while sharing cartons of Chinese as often as they'd fucked.

He'd also been one of the few to manage the feat of capturing her heart. Her one and only foray into how to do everything wrong. She'd fallen in love with her best friend. But back then Gabe had been focused on his career. He'd always given her the impression that their relationship was nothing more than friendship and casual sex to him. He'd proven it when he'd walked out of her life and never looked back.

That he was standing by the beach—the exact spot where she was supposed to meet her date—looking around him as if he were waiting on someone, made her stomach tighten. Was he tonight's date? Was it even possible?

The thought made her stomach flip-flop. In delicious anticipation. In nerves. In outright fear. What she *wanted* was to turn around and go home. Neither could she deny that curiosity had her by the heart. She'd thought of him often over the years, and just seeing him had all those questions roaring to the surface all over again. Where he was and what his life was like. The questions beating the hardest in the back of her mind, though, were of the more dangerous sort. Why he'd simply stopped contacting her and what she'd do if she ever saw him again.

Well, if he *was* her date tonight, she'd face it head-on, because Steph Mason didn't run from anything.

She drew her shoulders back, plastered on her best "no care in the world" smile, and sauntered in his direction. "Gabriel Donovan."

His head snapped in her direction, and familiar hazel eyes settled on her. Oh, she didn't have to see them to know their color. She'd know those eyes anywhere, because she'd spent years trying not to stare at them. Beautiful and intense, they were a mix of chocolate brown and a deep mossy green. They widened as recognition dawned over him. "Stephanie Mason. I'll be damned."

As she came to a stop in front of him, she had to tip her head back to look into his face. He stood a good head above her, and she shivered with the power of that broad body.

"The last time I saw you, you were crawling out of my bed." She attempted to keep the conversation light, but the truth was, Gabe had gotten a phone call that night that had changed his entire world. His parents had died a tragic, senseless death, literally at the wrong place at the wrong time. A robbery attempt gone wrong had left him suddenly in charge of his teenaged sister. Gabe had dropped out of school a week later and moved home to Oregon to take care of Molly.

"Been a long time, Steph." He grinned, revealing a dazzling smile that eleven years ago would have taken her breath away. Now it sent more memories flooding through her mind. That smile had drawn her in the first time he'd flashed it at her.

"That it has. Your last letter said you'd joined the military, that they were stationing you in California." They'd kept in touch for about a year after he'd gone home, but after he'd joined the military she'd stopped hearing from him.

He gave an absentminded nod. "Camp Coronado. It's where I did my BUD/S training."

Buds training... Where had she heard that term before? Wait a minute... "You were a SEAL?"

He darted a glance at her. "Mm-hmm. Team three. Moved back here about four years ago."

She nudged him with an elbow. "Seriously impressive."

He didn't say anything, but seemed to draw within himself. His gaze slid off to his right, and awkward tension moved over him. She searched her thoughts for something, anything, to pull him out of what seemed to be heavy thoughts, when her gaze settled on his tie. The sapphire blue stood out against the stark white of his shirt.

Her stomach sank into her stilettos. Damn. That tie meant Gabe *was* her date.

Well, the only thing to do now was face it. The way she did everything.

She drew a deep breath for courage and tugged on his tie. "Blue."

His gaze snapped back to her, dropped to his tie, then returned to her again. One corner of his mouth hitched. He nodded in her direction, no doubt indicating the similar color of her shirt. Amusement and recognition glinted in his eyes. "Also blue."

"That makes you the date I've been waiting for." She couldn't be sure if she wanted to hug the stuffing out of him or puke on his shoes.

He reached up to rub the back of his neck and glanced

around him. "Sorry I'm late. Forgot what part of the park we were supposed to meet at. I swore I wrote it down, but I couldn't find the damn note."

She lifted a brow. "Nervous?"

For that one small thing, she was eternally grateful. At least she wasn't the only one coming out of her skin. She'd been fine with her first real date since her breakup with Alec...right up until she'd realized they'd matched her with Gabe. She hadn't anticipated the power of being in his presence again, either.

He let out an uncomfortable laugh. "Does it show?"

"Nope. You're as solid as ever. Don't feel bad. The thought of this date has had my knees shaking all day." Aiming for light and upbeat, to not let him know seeing him again had unnerved her, she punched him lightly in the shoulder. "How the hell are you?"

"I'm good." Gabe laughed, his gaze sweeping the length of her. "You haven't changed a bit. Still as sexy as ever. The hair's changed, though. You had a pixie cut last I saw you. Long looks good on you."

The husky timbre of his voice made her nipples tighten. Whether consciously or otherwise, he reached out and pushed her hair back off her shoulder, his fingers brushing the skin of her neck. A full-out shiver swept the length of her spine, landing straight in her panties. God, she was doomed. One touch from him and her body lit up like a firework on the Fourth of July.

"You're still the same. Same curls." She reached up, fingering a lock of hair curling over his collar. "Same crooked smile."

He had lines around his eyes now that weren't there eleven years ago, but she had to admit she liked them. They lent his appearance a maturity that looked good on him. As if it were possible for Gabe Donovan to get any sexier.

A ghost of a smile flitted across his mouth, there and gone in the blink of an eye. His mouth formed a thin, grim line, and his jaw tightened.

She frowned, trying to comprehend the sudden tension moving over him. That was the second time in five minutes he'd gotten that look on his face. It was subtle but undeniable. Did he have PTSD like Trent? Was he remembering something?

Before she could ask if he was okay, though, he smiled again, this one tight and forced but polite all the same. "How 'bout we go get some dinner?"

She nodded. "Sounds great."

She shouldn't. History reminded her that nothing with Gabe would ever be what she wanted or needed at this point in her life. After all, she'd been little more to him than great sex. The way he'd walked out of her life and not looked back had proven that. He was here, though, and she couldn't deny that she'd been dying for eleven years to catch up with him.

While she was at it, maybe he'd share what was on his mind, and maybe she'd finally get the answers to all those questions he'd left her with.

CHAPTER TWO

I can't believe you still ride." A measure of awe filled her voice as Steph circled his bike.

Standing several feet away, hands stuffed in his pockets, Gabe grunted in acknowledgment. He'd become caught in watching *her*. When he'd suggested dinner, his intention had been to distract her. Her innocent comment about change had brought up the ugly reminder that at some point he was going to have to talk about his leg. Going into this date, he'd known the subject would have to come up, but having to tell Steph, given everything they'd shared and the way their relationship had ended, only made it harder.

Then they'd come out here to the parking lot. She'd taken one look at his bike and grinned so wide it had nearly split her face in half. God, of all the women Military Match could have paired him with, it had to be her. She was still gorgeous, too. The same flirty smile that made her eyes light up. The same supple curves and firm, tight ass. Her dirty-blond hair fell past her shoulders now, thick and straight, and he itched to sift his hands through it, for the luxury of feeling the soft strands slip through his fingers. He knew every spot on her long, slender neck that made her shiver and every spot on her body that made her moan. Hell, there wasn't an inch of her his mouth *hadn't* skimmed at some point.

Now here she was, standing before him like temptation itself. How many times over the years had he wished for this moment? That he'd have the chance to tell her all those things he should have told her years ago?

Steph glanced back at him as she stroked her fingers over the black leather seat, following the lines of stitching. "Whatever happened to that bike you had in college?"

He shrugged. "Sold it and upgraded."

"Can't see you with flames, though." One corner of her mouth hitched upward as she traced her fingers over the orange and red flames on the tank. "I always saw you as a simple kind of guy. Just black and chrome."

Gabe chuckled as another, more recent, memory filled his mind. The day he'd bought the bike. It had been the first anniversary of Julia's death, and he'd wanted to do something positive for Char by letting her help him pick out the colors and designs. She'd insisted it needed flames. "Those were Char's idea."

Shit. Heart hammering like a freight train, he dragged a shaking hand through his hair. He hadn't meant to tell her about Char yet, hadn't even thought about when or how to tell her. He hadn't a clue what to expect from his date tonight, whether or not she'd have a problem with him being a single father, and had hoped he could put the conversation off until later. Like with his leg, though, telling Steph was a whole other ball of wax. It came with a story instinct told him she wouldn't like.

Steph, as usual, didn't miss a beat. As she rounded the front wheel, her gaze flicked to him, her brows raised in curiosity. "Char?"

His stomach lurched. He'd have to face this eventually. Now, he supposed, was as good a time as any. So he put on the proudest smile he could muster and prayed for a miracle. "Short for Charlotte. My daughter."

Her eyes widened with surprise, like it was the most absurd idea she'd ever heard. "*You* have a daughter?"

Dread sank in his stomach like a heavy lead weight. Was that good or bad? "Char's ten. She came as quite a surprise to me, too, when I found out. Now I can't imagine my life without her."

Steph blinked, stared for a beat, eyes searching. Waiting for her reaction tied his gut into knots on top of knots. Was she doing the math? Figuring out that Char had been born almost exactly a year after he'd left Seattle, a mere two months after the last time he'd seen *her*?

She didn't slap him or turn around and storm off, the way he'd always envisioned. The way he deserved. Rather, she smiled. It didn't quite reach her eyes, but it rang with sweetness all the same. "Look at you all grown up. Got any pictures?"

"Later. Come on. I'm starved." He unstrapped the spare helmet and handed it to her, then swung a leg over the seat and pulled the bike upright, releasing the kickstand.

He had a dozen pictures of Char packed into his wallet, but he had no desire to show her. At least not now. When he did, she'd invariably ask where Char's mother was, and he'd have to tell her. He didn't want to think about Julia right now, let alone talk about her. If he had to explain this now, the guilt would eat at him. He'd make an excuse and go home. He wanted things with her he wasn't sure were his to want. Companionship. Sex.

Memories of their time together taunted him. When he'd arrived ten minutes ago, his nerves had been in his throat. Standing beside the lake, searching the darkened path for his faceless date, he wasn't sure he could even do it. A date yes. That was easy. But sex?

And then he'd caught sight of Steph. Right then he only knew two things for sure. She was still gorgeous, and her smile still lit a flame in his gut. For now that had to be enough. Oh, he wanted her. Even eleven years later, it was still there, the desire that had drawn them together in the first place. It was the sensual glint in her eyes, and he ached to dive into her, simply to lose the grief and loneliness his life had become in her sweet, soft body. Let her soothe his soul the way she had once upon a time.

Because she had. It was what had always made him feel so guilty every time he thought about her over the years. What kind of husband did that make him when he'd thought about someone he'd shared so much with while married to Julia?

He also couldn't give her forever now any more than he could in college, and Steph deserved better. Always had. For now he'd concentrate on catching up with a friend.

When she didn't climb on behind him, he turned his head. She stood staring at him, melancholy filling her blue eyes. Whatever went on inside that pretty little head of hers scared the hell out of him, because the desire to ask, to fall back into old routines with her, was strong. It had always been so easy with her.

So he held out a hand instead. "You coming?"

She nodded, put on the helmet and fastened the chin strap, then accepted his hand and climbed on behind him. For a split second she froze, then rested her chin on his shoulder. Her hands slid around his rib cage exactly the way they used to. "I missed you, you know."

The same melancholy he'd seen in her eyes filled her voice and hit him square in the chest. He had the sudden, over-whelming desire to stroke her thigh, the way he might have once upon a time, for the simple need to connect with her. In-stead, he took a moment to pull out his keys.

"Time got away from me. I always meant to catch up with you, but life got...busy. Molly went to college, and after Char was born, I enlisted..." He shrugged, the words he knew he needed to say clogging his throat. He had so many things he'd always sworn he'd tell her if ever he had the chance. That he'd never realized how important she was to him until she was no longer a part of his life, because he'd been too damn caught up in himself, in all those lofty plans he'd had for his career.

How sorry he was that he hadn't kept in touch. She'd been his best friend, and he'd simply let her go. Of all his regrets, Steph was a big one.

"It's okay." She patted the side of her seat. "Come on. Start this beast. I want to hear it growl. We can catch up over dinner."

* * *

Twenty minutes later, they sat in a booth at a small Thai place a few blocks from the park, waiting for dinner to be served. Across from him, Steph sipped a tiny porcelain cup of jasmine tea. Gabe attempted to focus on her and not the busy restaurant around him. Since he'd left the service, his PTSD had lessened to a large degree, but he still had trouble with busy crowds.

Steph set her teacup on the table and folded her hands together, her blue gaze piercing and intense. "You always were a brooder. From the looks of you over there, you haven't changed much. What're you thinking?"

He grimaced and dropped his gaze to his own, untouched, cup of tea. Apparently, he wasn't holding it together very well. Some date he was.

"I'm sorry. The restaurant is full, and being in a crowd still makes me a little antsy. They seated us in the center of the room. There's nothing solid behind me." He shrugged, trying to play it off, to not sound as pathetic as he felt. "It's still an instinct to want to protect my back."

Not sitting with his back to the wall had every nerve ending pulsing like a live wire, and his senses expanded, homed in on every damn sound around him. Every chink of silverware or sudden burst of laughter was a grenade going off. It made his head pound and his heart hammer like a freight train.

She smiled. "Don't worry, big guy. I've got your back."

The knot in his gut relaxed a fraction. He'd always loved that about her, her understanding, forgiving nature. "I appreciate that. I have to admit I also haven't done this in a while. I have no idea what to say to you."

She glanced down, twirling the ceramic cup between her fingers. "So is this officially a date, then? I'd just assumed we were old friends catching up."

"I'm not altogether sure. Either way, eleven years is a long time." And there was a lot of water under this bridge.

"Well, for what it's worth, you're not alone there. I'm not sure what to say to you, either." She lifted her tea, peering at him over the rim as she took another sip. "Can I ask why you're here? Why a dating service, I mean?"

He let out a quiet laugh, grateful for the subject change. That, at least, was an easy question. "Because Char and Molly tell me it's time."

She stared at him for a beat, shrewd eyes working his face. Seconds later, her eyes filled with an empathy that caught him in the chest. "You lost someone."

His whole body tensed as he tried to prepare himself for the reaction to come. The one reaction that, while kind and expected, still felt like pouring salt into an open wound. "My wife died three years ago."

Steph put a hand to her mouth, her eyes filling with the exact look he'd feared: the pity and concern. "Oh, Gabe..."

When her hand shot across the table, he yanked his out of reach and clenched his teeth until his jaw ached. "Don't."

If one more person told him how sorry they were he'd come unglued. All the sorry in the world didn't bring Julia back or make it any easier to pick up and move on. Molly was right. It had been three years. He wanted—needed—to move on. Knowing that didn't make it easy. Even three years later, he still had trouble.

Grief squeezed at his chest, so tight he had to force himself to inhale. Right behind it came the anger he didn't know what to do with, the desperate desire to put his fist through something. Seated across the table from Steph, of all people, only compounded the guilt eating at his stomach.

Steph stared for a moment, then pulled her hand back slowly. She sat stiffly, looking down at her tea. "I'm sorry."

He blew out a pent-up breath, forcing himself to release the emotions along with it. "No, I'm the one who's sorry. Obviously, it's still a sore spot. It's really hard to forget and move on when people give you that look."

She glanced up, eyes full of remorse and understanding. "You still miss her."

"'Cause that's what you want to hear your date tell you, right?" He let out a bitter laugh and shoved shaking fingers through his hair, pulling his bangs off his forehead. "Sorry, Steph. I'm not sure this was a good idea."

The waitress arrived then, and tense silence rose over the table as she set their plates in front of them. Steph dug into hers and Gabe followed suit, grateful for a moment to collect himself. Except they ate in silence for too damn long. The Panang curry he'd ordered was good, the sauce smooth and creamy with a slightly spicy kick, the chicken tender. Not that he cared.

Finally, Steph set down her fork and sat back. She studied him, her shrewd gaze, like always, seeming to see right through him. After a moment, she set her elbows on the table and steepled her fingers. "Can I ask you something?"

He picked up his fork and concentrated on stirring the pile of rice into the spicy sauce on his plate. He hated avoiding her, but he had no desire to know what played in her eyes or discover what she'd seen in his. "I just bit your head off for being nice. I'm pretty sure that earns you the right to ask anything you want."

She remained silent a moment, but her intense gaze burned into him. Finally, she reached across the table, laying her hand over his wrist. "Gabe, look at me."

He blew out a heavy breath and did as she asked. He owed her that much at least. What he found in her gaze, however, wasn't what he'd expected. Her brows furrowed, blue eyes stern. A look he well recognized. Steph was about to get her lecture on. God, she really hadn't changed.

She squeezed his wrist. "It's okay."

He gripped his fork tight in his fist with the frustration winding through him. "No. It's not."

Never one to be deterred, she pulled her hand back, only to set it on the table, palm up. What she wanted was clear as day, but damned if he could bring himself to set his hand in hers. It would be a connection, not only to another human being, but to *her*. A woman he'd relied on once, whose body he'd know by feel in the darkest of rooms. It didn't matter how many times he told himself it was okay, normal even. After all, Julia was gone; she'd want him to move on. Had told him as much. It still felt like cheating.

Steph wiggled her fingers in insistence.

He gave in. When her soft fingers closed around his, something inside of him sighed, the relief so profound the tension in his chest finally eased.

She set her other hand on top, encompassing his fingers in the warmth of hers. "It's okay."

He frowned and shook his head. "I still don't agree, but thank you. You had a question."

Her thumb stroked his palm. Idle. Torturous. That single stroke shuddered through him, lighting up every nerve ending along the way, and for a moment he could only stare at her slender fingers. It had been so long since a woman had touched him that way. With tenderness. With care. It filled a need he'd forgotten about and created a dozen more. Christ. Did Steph have any idea how badly he needed that touch?

"Now, how 'bout you give me the real reason you're here."

Her softly spoken comment pulled him out of his reverie, and he looked up at her. He found himself answering honestly and praying, somehow, she'd understand. The way she used to. "Ever want something you can't pin down?"

A slow smile slid across her face. "Yeah."

He focused on her familiar blue eyes and let them give him the courage to say what he needed her to know. "Molly's been bugging me. She says it's time I moved on, and to a certain extent, she's right. I don't do well on my own. The nights..."

He shook his head, at a loss to explain any further, and shifted his gaze to the other side of the restaurant, watching for a moment as a waitress set plates in front of an elderly couple. How the hell did he explain something that didn't make much sense to him either?

"Are too long."

Steph's words drifted across the table at barely a murmur, but she might as well have shouted them. Surprised once again by the understanding in her tone, he turned his head. Having released his hand, she now dug through her pad thai noodles, her gaze on her plate, but her cheeks flushed. Only someone who went to bed alone every night could possibly understand the loneliness it left in your chest. To know *she* went to bed that way set his teeth grinding together. Earlier, he'd been too surprised at discovering she was his date to really think about it. Then he'd gotten lost in the past.

Now a million questions filled his mind. Like why she wasn't married yet. Or why she needed a dating service in the first place. It also relit that flame in his gut. The desire. He longed to fall into her again, to wrap his body around her and lose himself in her touch. Despite hoping otherwise, he hadn't expected to feel desire for his date tonight. With Steph, that fire flared all too easily. The problem was, he wasn't sure he could be anything she needed.

Which meant that wherever this night led them, whatever her expectations for this date, she deserved to know where he stood.

He folded his hands on the table. "You asked earlier if this was a date. I suppose I should be honest with you. I'm not looking for anything permanent."

She looked up, brows raised in surprise. A beat later she sobered, offering him a soft smile. "Relax, Gabe. No pressure. Tell me about your daughter."

He scooped another bite of the curry and stuffed it in his mouth, using the task to try to cool his jets. He didn't want to talk about Char. All he could think about was Steph, about how badly she made his cock ache.

It was time to distract her or he'd lose his mind.

"Your turn. Why the need for a dating service?" He darted a glance at her as he scooped another forkful of the curry.

"Sorry, but I just can't see it. The Stephanie Mason I knew was an incorrigible flirt."

Her fork paused halfway to her mouth. She held it there for a moment before setting it down on her plate. "You want the truth or the fluff version?"

He gave a half-hearted shrug. *Hell, let's go for broke.* "The truth."

Her gaze locked on his, bold and unapologetic, but her throat bobbed.

"I've done the whole one-night fling thing for too long now. I want...something different. I want someone who'll remember my name, who wants more than just a night of great sex." Just as quickly as her boldness had come, she dropped her gaze to her plate, pushing her food around but never really accomplishing anything. "Someone worth waking up to."

The hurt she couldn't quite hide seeped into her tone. Irritation punched him hard in the stomach and bristled along his nerve endings. He'd always hoped she was happy and settled. Obviously, there was a wound in there somewhere, and he had the sudden urge to deck the asshole responsible for it.

"And you haven't."

Like someone had drawn the shades over her, the look disappeared. Steph straightened in her seat and forked a bite of noodles but wouldn't look at him. "Not yet. Truth is, I haven't allowed myself to."

He followed her lead for the moment and concentrated on his plate. If she wasn't comfortable sharing, he wouldn't push. They ate in unbearable silence, and the knowledge slowly drove him insane. He hated the thought of someone hurting her to the degree that she'd closed herself off. It was a lonely way to live.

Unable to stand it, he set down his fork and looked up at her. "Why haven't you?"

She stared at him for a beat, then made a show of pouring herself another cup of tea, stirring in a teaspoon of sugar, then taking a sip. Finally, she shrugged.

"I made a fool of myself for a man once. For a while I was determined never to make that mistake again. But it's lonely, and I hate sleeping alone. Hate waking up to a stranger even more." She set down her tea and pinned him with a direct, focused stare. "Your turn. What did *you* hope to get out of this date?"

"I wanted...something in the middle. A first step. I'm not sure I'm ready for something permanent again yet, but I'd like something more than a one-night stand. I'm human. I don't like being alone, either." He huffed a laugh. "Sex might be nice. You know, with someone besides myself."

For the second time that night, the words left his mouth unbidden, and Gabe's gut clenched. He dragged a hand through his hair. Christ. Eleven years might have passed, but apparently she still had it, that certain something he'd never been able to resist that had him telling her all his damn secrets.

A slow grin curled across Steph's face, lightening the heavy emotion in her eyes. "There's that painfully blunt guy I used to know."

His cheeks blazed, but he couldn't help his echoing grin. "What? I thought we were being honest."

She laughed, so long and hard she sagged back against her

seat. Gabe sat stunned, watching her. Her whole face lit up. The warmth radiating from her like the freakin' sun drew him in like a bee to a bright yellow flower.

Steph's giggling died away. She dropped her gaze to her plate, a soft pink flush suffusing her cheeks. "You're staring."

He jerked his gaze to his plate, pushing the food around. "Sorry. I forgot how beautiful you are when you laugh like that."

He'd forgotten a lot of things about her. Like how much he enjoyed the simple act of sitting in the same room with her. For a few minutes she made him forget the lonely ache in his chest. Here, with her, he was simply a man out for a night with a beautiful woman. He didn't know a lot of things these days. Like where this date ought to go, or even where he wanted it to go.

What he did know was he didn't want to be sitting here, holed up in this crowded, noisy restaurant, when he could be doing a thousand other things with her.

Running with the thought, he set down his fork and met her gaze. "Let's get the hell out of here."

Steph blinked. Then she furrowed her brow and shook her head. "Where to?"

"Beats the hell out of me. I'm not even sure I care, but I have a sore need to get lost for a while." He reached into his back pocket for his wallet, pulled out his debit card, and raised his hand, flagging down their waitress. When she smiled in acknowledgment, he turned back to Steph, holding his hand out, palm up, on the table. "Get lost with me."

CHAPTER THREE

Steph stared at Gabe's outstretched hand, at the hopeful expression on his face and the light in those gorgeous hazel eyes. She had a feeling if she let herself, she'd follow him anywhere for the chance to relive—even temporarily—what they used to share.

The problem was, nothing with Gabe would ever be simple or uncomplicated. Even if she decided to stray from her plan to find a more lasting relationship, he was a widower, his heart still under lock and key, and she'd loved him once. Eleven years ago, their friendship had ended abruptly, leaving her to pick up the pieces of a broken heart. Oh, she'd understood why. His parents' deaths had forced him into a situation he couldn't possibly have prepared for. And clearly he'd gotten married, created a life for himself.

But the way he'd left had hurt all the same. Did she really want to travel this road with him again?

Gabe wiggled his fingers at her, amusement glinting in his eyes. The need to connect with him rose like an ancient ship from the depths of the ocean. She damn well knew she'd kill to spend time with him again.

"All right." She drew up straight and met his gaze. "So long as we get a few things straight first."

He studied her for a moment, gaze working her face, then folded his hands together on the table. "Go on."

Steph knotted her fingers. It was time to pull out *the rules*. She'd hoped she wouldn't need them for this date, wanting something more permanent. But with Gabe she needed all the armor she could muster. As a lawyer, she knew the importance of setting clear ground rules for even the most carefree adventure.

"Wherever this leads, it's temporary. I won't spend longer than a weekend with you. I don't want to get to know your daughter, either." She never did, because getting to know a man's family created messy things like emotions. But with Gabe it was a flat-out lie. She ached to see the girl, to know what she looked like. Did she look like him or her mother? "And I want nights. All night. I decided something when I signed up for this service. I won't be somebody's warm body anymore. I realize that'll be hard for you, given that you're a single father, but I just can't handle waking up alone anymore."

Gabe stared in silence. For so long, doubt began to creep over her. Had she been too demanding? Did she come off as the control freak she suddenly felt like?

Steph's cheeks flamed as the realization slid over, and she closed her eyes. God, she did sound like a control freak.

She swallowed her nerves and opened her eyes, ready to spew a thousand apologies, when Gabe's brow furrowed and his jaw tightened.

"I don't know who hurt you, but I'd really like to deck him." He reached across the table, capturing her hand. His thumb swept hers, and he held her gaze, voice softening. "Relax, Steph. I was thinking more along the lines of dessert, that maybe we'd wander the city together a bit."

She set her elbow on the table and dropped her forehead into her free hand. "I'm sorry. That was so off the wall. You struck a nerve, and I panicked."

"Well, now we're even." He chuckled and turned her hand over, sweeping her knuckles with his thumb. "Who was he?"

She sighed. "His name was Alec. He was a partner at the law firm I worked at. Three years together, and he finally asked me to marry him." The memory rose over her, her humiliation flooding right behind it. "The day of, I was at the church, dressed and waiting, when he texted to tell me he wasn't coming. He sent me a freakin' text—can you believe it?"

The waitress arrived with their check then, and Gabe turned away briefly to hand her his card. "He was an ass, and he did you a favor."

Steph swirled her teacup on the table. "Agreed, but obviously it's left a mark."

Gabe blinked solemnly at her. "Not all of us are like that, you know."

She wasn't sure she agreed but bit her tongue. Those kinds of men were all she'd found. Sadly, including him. In fact, he'd been the first one to show her how easily men could leave her. And if she'd learned her lesson the first time, she never would have been humiliated by Alec. Though, really, she had only herself to blame for never telling Gabe she loved him. If only she'd dug up the nerve back then to share her feelings, would things have turned out differently between them?

Their waitress returned with the receipt. Gabe slid from his chair and held out his hand. "Come on. Let's go find dessert."

She set her hand in his and let him pull her to her feet. They left the restaurant, walking in silence for a while down the busy Seattle street. People were still out in droves, enjoying the unusually nice weather. The more they walked, the more the tension from earlier dissipated. The ease she'd always felt with him followed them. Even after all this time apart, there was no need for forced conversation. A smile or glance said it all.

It was wonderful and amazing and absolutely terrifying.

A couple blocks down, a familiar shop came into view. She glanced at Gabe. "Since you picked up the tab for dinner, dessert's on me. I know a great little bakery. It's just down the street."

Gabe stopped on the sidewalk and stared at her for a long, unnerving moment. His gaze worked her face, as if he were deciding something. Finally, he drew a deep breath and released it. "You know, we could always take it back to my place. I've got the house to myself until Sunday morning."

Steph's heart hammered. He hadn't said the words, but his invitation blinked at her like a neon bulb. His eyes filled with a gleam she'd seen so times in the past she knew it almost by heart. Hunger so intense a shiver slid through her in response. Her knees wobbled, and her core throbbed. God. Eleven years, and he still had the power to make her wet with a single glance.

Saying yes would be impetuous, of course, and everything

36 JM Stewart

she'd sworn she'd stop doing when she'd signed up with Military Match. Yet his offer was irresistible. Gabe wasn't *any* lover. The man made her toes curl. The last time they made love, he'd left her breathless and spent and closer to him than any man she'd dated up until that point.

What harm could a weekend do?

She smiled and nodded. "Sounds good. Come on."

She turned back to the street and they started off again. If she didn't focus on her destination, she'd either drag him into a dark corner and plaster her mouth on his or talk herself out of going home with him. Luckily, Gabe didn't press further but walked quietly beside her.

At the end of the block, she pushed into the familiar shop. Lauren's Chocolates and Pastries sat at the end of the row, surrounded by stores with everything from jewelry to books. Inside the entrance, a three-foot-tall wooden bear carrying a white wedding cake grinned at her. Trent had given it to Lauren on her last birthday. That bear made Steph feel at home every time she entered.

"Friend of mine owns this place." Steph released Gabe's arm and headed for the register, where Elise, Lauren's assistant, was boxing up chocolates for another customer. She smiled as Elise looked up. "Hi, Elise. She around?"

Please say no. Between her two best friends, Lauren was the quiet, shy one of the bunch. She'd still tease her, though, and while she wasn't sure she could handle the, albeit good-natured, ribbing right now, Lauren's bakery was the best in the city. She'd put up with the possible humiliation to get her hands on some of Lauren's incredible chocolate-chocolate chip cookies. They were her guilty pleasure.

"Hello, hello! No. I'm afraid not. She took off about an hour ago." Elise looked up and flashed a smile that lit up her whole face.

Elise was in her midfifties, though you couldn't tell by the dark shade of her hair. Hair she insisted she hadn't dyed to cover gray. She had the kind of disposition Steph envied, always so cheerful and friendly. No matter how bad of a day Steph was having, coming in here and chatting with Elise always pulled her out of her funk.

Now her smile did exactly that—relaxed the knot in Steph's stomach. She blew out her held breath. For sure when this weekend was over, she'd need a gabfest with Lauren and Mandy, but she didn't want to do it now, while on a first date. And a blind one at that, with a man she had a long, complicated history with.

"I know this place."

Gabe's voice sounded behind her, full of awe and recognition. Steph turned a confused frown on him. "You do?"

Halfway up the shop, he'd stopped to look around him. His gaze landed on her again, and he headed in her direction. "My detailer's girl owns this place."

It took her all of two seconds to understand what he told her.

"Oh my God. You're *that* Gabe." Lauren's fiancé, Trent, worked as a detailer slash mechanic in a custom motorcycle shop. The few times they'd all gotten together, she'd heard him mention his boss, Gabe, but she'd never thought anything of it. There had to be a thousand Gabes in Seattle, right?

Suddenly the world seemed a whole lot smaller.

A slow grin curled across Gabe's face, like he'd arrived at the same conclusion she had. He waved his fingers in the air, singing, "It's a small world, after all."

A giggle popped out of her. She'd forgotten that side of him, the playful guy who could still be a great big kid.

Gabe's grin widened. He sidled up to the counter beside her and set his hands on the surface. "So, what's good?"

Elise, proud baker and worth every penny Lauren paid her, winked. "Everything."

Gabe chuckled.

"Give us a dozen. Make it a mix." Steph waved a hand in the air. "Surprise me."

"You got it, honey." Elise smiled and turned to pull a white bakery box from the counter behind her, then moved down the display case.

Gabe moved with her. For every item, Elise would point, then arch a brow at him, and Gabe would either frown and shake his head or give her a thumb's-up. Several of Lauren's gourmet truffles went into the box, along with a decadent cupcake and several cookies. Steph lost track after that.

The dozen complete several minutes later, they moved back to the register. Gabe hip-bumped Steph out of the way and pulled out his wallet. When she opened her mouth to protest, he winked at her.

"My treat. Because I can." When Elise handed him back his card, he smiled, giving her a two-fingered salute. "Have a good night."

As he grabbed Steph's arm and headed for the front entrance, Elise grinned and waved a hand at her face, mouthing, *Hot!*

Steph swallowed her tongue trying to hold back her giggle and waved instead. "Bye, Elise."

For sure, Elise would tell Lauren she'd stopped by with her date, no doubt giving her the lowdown on Gabe, but Steph couldn't care less at this point. The girls would pounce on her tomorrow anyway.

They walked in silence again, returning to where he'd left his bike in the restaurant parking lot. He released her arm, moved to the rear and tied the box to the back with the same mesh bungee the spare helmet had been strapped down with. Once finished, he turned to her. Despite his playfulness inside the bakery, something somber played in his eyes as he tucked his fingertips into his pockets. "So, my place, right?"

She turned fully to face him. As she stared up into those eyes, her stomach wobbled. God, it still amazed her. When she'd decided to go along with Mandy to this dating service, she'd been bound and determined to do things differently. To take things slower than her normal routine. That her date ended up being Gabe had thrown her for a loop. As sure as she stood there, all those old emotions crept over her, and the part of her that refused to get hurt again screamed to get the hell out now.

All of which meant she hadn't a clue where this was going. She only knew she couldn't resist him now any more than she could eleven years ago.

"That's the second time you asked me that. It tells me you're nervous, which makes me curious . . ." Drawing a deep breath, she laid a trembling hand against his chest. He was still as warm as she remembered, like he had his own internal space heater. "What do you want from this, Gabe?"

Heat flared in his eyes, answering the question, but he gave her a gentle smile all the same. "I could ask you the same thing."

Her insides wobbled again, and all sensation pooled between her thighs. Oh, she could deny it, but she knew damn well what she wanted. Him. Preferably naked beneath her. If she remembered correctly, he preferred the cowgirl position. The very thought of hugging his lean hips and sliding onto his thick erection nearly wrenched a needy moan from her throat.

She offered him a playful smile. "That's a non-answer."

The corners of his mouth twitched. "So is that."

He took a step closer, staring for a beat, a silent communication they'd shared a thousand times before. Anticipation sizzled through her blood. Then he cupped her face in the warmth of his palms and settled his mouth over hers. Steph sighed into the connection. Damn it, she couldn't help herself. His kiss was everything she remembered and then some. A gentle tangle of lips and a soft stroke of his tongue. Her mouth fell open of its own accord, and she pressed her body into his before she even realized she'd moved.

By the time he finally pulled back enough to meet her gaze, her knees had turned to Jell-O and her panties were drenched. She'd have followed him anywhere.

He gave her a tender smile and lifted a hand, stroking the shell of her ear as he tucked away a lock of hair. Those intense eyes worked her face, his body trembling against her. "That was familiar, huh?"

She let out a breathless laugh and dropped her forehead to his chest. "Your kiss still packs one hell of a punch."

His quiet laugh rumbled through his chest as he wrapped his big arms around her, pulling her tight against him. He went silent, holding her, and for that brief moment she allowed herself to get lost again in the luxurious feel of being in his arms. How could it be that even eleven years later, he still had that addicting pull over her? Like the time hadn't passed at all, one kiss, one touch, and she crumbled to his whim. His to take. She'd need to be careful if she wanted to make it out of this weekend with her heart still intact.

Which meant she needed to redraw her boundaries.

"So we're in agreement, then? This is just for the weekend?" She couldn't allow herself to get caught up in him again. "I won't deny I want this. You. But I need it to stay short-lived."

He nodded, his warm hands working her back, slowly stroking up and down her spine, driving her to distraction. "I know the way I left must seem rather...callous to you. We can talk about that later if you want."

She smiled, relieved he understood. "Sounds good."

He released her, mounting his bike and pulling it upright. Steph climbed on behind him and allowed herself the luxury of wrapping her arms around him. If she only had until Sunday morning, she intended to enjoy him.

* * *

They arrived back at the park five minutes later. For a moment neither one moved. Steph loathed the thought of letting him go. She'd always loved riding with him. Sitting with her arms around him, the wind roaring past her helmet. Now it gave her a chance to be close to him after so many years spent missing him.

With a deep breath, she forced herself to let go, climbed off the bike, and unstrapped the box of goodies, tucking it under one arm. He restrapped the extra helmet to the back, then stood facing her. "Follow me? I'm in Redmond. Let's hope there's no traffic."

She nodded. Instead of climbing back on his bike, though, Gabe stood staring at her. The odd look she remembered from earlier crossed his features again. Somber and broody. As if something heavy weighed on his mind he was trying to decide whether to share.

He confirmed her suspicions when he tucked his hands in his pockets, something she recalled him doing often back in college. "There's something you're going to need to know about me. Something I need to show you. I'd rather do it at home, though, if that's all right."

She searched his face. "Is it bad? 'Cause you look nervous again."

He let out a quiet laugh and reached up to rub the back of his neck. "I am. It's not something I tell people often, but if we're spending the weekend together, you'll need to know, because it's unavoidable."

She laid a hand against his chest. "Whatever it is, I'm sure it'll be fine. Come on. Let's go."

When he nodded, she moved around her car and climbed behind the wheel, setting their dessert in the passenger seat.

A half hour later, she pulled up behind him in a long driveway. Steph eyed the house as she grabbed the box of goodies and climbed from the car. He owned a small rambler, painted a beautiful shade of fern green. The porch was set back from the walkway so that it resembled an alcove. Seated beside the door was a small rocking chair, behind it a single window that somehow added to the hominess of the place.

Gabe, keys in hand, came to stop beside her and hooked his thumbs in his pockets. "Home sweet home."

Steph turned to eye the neighborhood around them again and tossed him a teasing smile. "Gabe Donovan, you live in suburbia."

The entire neighborhood sat back off the main road in one of the many prefabricated housing developments that had begun cropping up all over the place. The houses were all of similar sizes and colors, every lawn, including his, perfectly groomed, each backyard hidden by a six-foot privacy fence. Gabe's place sat at the end of a cul-de-sac that came complete with a basketball hoop lined up in the semicircular road.

Gabe rolled his eyes, one corner of his mouth hitching as he turned toward the house, making his way to the front door.

"I'm a single father. Where did you expect me to live? Some of us"—he shoved the key into the dead bolt lock and shot a crooked grin over his shoulder—"have actually grown up."

That sexy grin sent a riotous mass of butterflies fluttering in her stomach. Her palms grew sweaty. She'd forgotten that, too, the addicting playfulness of being with him, how easy it was.

He shoved the door open, stepped inside, and turned to the wall on the left, hitting a light switch and illuminating the interior.

Steph swallowed a sudden case of nerves and followed him

inside, stepping up onto a colorful welcome mat. "I may have gotten older, Gabe, but I refuse to grow up."

He closed the door behind her and stood studying her. His gorgeous hazel eyes glittered with amusement and filled with heat. "You haven't changed."

Her stomach dipped and swayed like a high school girl staring up at her first love. All she could see, all she wanted to see, was him. Oh, how she used to love being against that broad body. What was it about a big man that made her shiver all over?

She offered a friendly smile, hoping to cover the reaction she couldn't contain. "You have."

"That's what happens when you have kids." He jerked his head toward the interior and turned, moving farther into the house. "Come on."

They stepped out of the three-by-five hallway that served as the foyer and emerged into the main room of the house. The kitchen, living room, and dining room all formed one large, open space. Gabe led her off to the kitchen on the right.

Steph stopped at the island separating the kitchen from the living room, set the bakery box on the counter, and turned to take in the space. The house had a definite woman's flair. Maroon decorative throw pillows sat tucked into each corner of the tan sofa, and elegant gold lamps sat on the mahogany end tables. The pièce de résistance, though, were the opaque white curtains covering the sliding glass doors. No man she'd been with had ever bothered with curtains, Gabe included.

Back in college, she never would've pictured him here, but she had to admit the place had a certain charm. She wanted a house like this someday, and the family to fill it. If she was ever going to get that life, she needed to banish her defense mechanisms. Otherwise she'd be alone forever.

She took a seat at the breakfast bar. "Nice place."

He moved around the opposite side of the island and laid his hands on the surface, that lone corner of his mouth hitching. "You sound surprised."

She shrugged. "I still see you in that studio apartment you had at U Dub. No headboard on the bed, a beat-up old sofa."

He glanced around, melancholy seeming to hang on him for a moment. "Julia's handiwork. I've gotten used to it."

At the mention of his wife, her heart did a little clench. Getting a glimpse into what his life with his wife had been like had the green-eyed monster roaring in her head.

She firmly ignored it. The woman was dead for crying out loud.

She chose, instead, to focus on him. After sliding from the stool, she moved around the counter and came to stand beside him. "I'm sorry about your wife."

Everything else aside, her chest ached for him and his daughter. She knew the pain of losing a parent. She'd lost her mother at the ripe old age of seven. Lost her father to the alcoholism that developed after Mom died. Dad was sober these days, living in a halfway house in Puyallup somewhere, but not by choice. Refusing to play the part of his enabler anymore, she'd had to let him sit in the mess he'd made of his life, and he resented her for it. He never called, and when she called him, he never had anything nice to say. She was essentially alone in the world.

"Thank you." Gabe looked over at her. A tiny crease formed between his brows as he frowned. A heartbeat later, he turned toward her and closed the distance between them. His scent swirled around her, his body heat infusing hers as he looped his hands around her waist and tugged her against him. "So. I should tell you now. Before we get too deep into this."

Simply being against his big, warm body had her shivering all over, heat dancing across the surface of her skin, but it was the intensity playing in his searching eyes that caught and held her attention. There was that look again.

"Why do I get the feeling this news is bad?" More to the point, why did the thought of it make her stomach drop?

He gave a slow shake of his head, his voice low and somber. "That depends entirely on you."

Hands caught between them, she rubbed slow circles over his chest, trying to soothe his obvious tension. "Whatever it is, maybe you should just get it over with. Like a Band-Aid. Rip it off quick."

He let out an uncomfortable huff of a laugh. "That's exactly what Marcus said."

"Now you're starting to scare me." She ducked down a bit in an effort to look into his eyes. "Gabe, what on earth is it?"

He finally looked up. His body trembled against her, but he held her gaze, bold and unapologetic. "You mentioned earlier that I hadn't changed much. Truth is, parts of me have."

CHAPTER FOUR

Gabe's heart hammered his rib cage. The way Steph stared at him, eyes wide and curious, waiting patiently for news he still wasn't sure he wanted to share, made his insides shake. It gave him the sensation of standing naked in front of a room full of people, like all his secrets were laid bare before her, which wasn't far from the truth.

When he'd agreed to this date, he hadn't anticipated *her*. Their history meant his mind and body had fast-forwarded. Or rewound, as the case was, sending him back into the past. One look at the heat in her eyes sent an inferno blazing through his veins. Eleven years might have passed, but his body remembered, responded to hers. He ached to have her naked beneath him.

Simply so he could lose himself in her touch. The way he used to. After losing his parents and Julia, along with all the ugly stuff he'd seen in the war, he needed it even more.

But before he could do any of that, he needed to tell her about his leg. If it bothered her, he'd rather know now.

Drawing a deep breath for courage, he slid his hand down his left thigh and inched his pant leg up enough to reveal the bottom half of his prosthetic. Then he waited, heart pounding in his throat.

Steph blinked, her brow furrowing, as if she didn't quite understand. A split second later, she gasped, her hand flying up to cover her mouth.

"Oh my God, Gabe. You lost your leg. How much did you lose?" She darted a glance at him but didn't wait for an answer and bent over, stroking her hand down his thigh. "When did this happen?"

He drew his shoulders back, curled his fingers around the keys in his pocket, and let her have the moment, feel as much as she needed to. Every muscle in his body tensed, from his shoulders right down to the thigh she was currently smoothing her palm over. A tight, hard ball of dread formed in his gut, threatening to bring his dinner back up as he waited for her to say something. It was the most vulnerable he'd felt since . . . hell. Since Julia died and he'd come to the stark realization he was now a single father.

After several moments Steph finally pulled her hand back and straightened. As she met his gaze again, the kitchen's overhead light glinted off tears slowly filling her eyes. Her lower lip wobbled. "H-how did it happen?"

Gabe leaned back against the counter beside her, pretending more fortitude than he felt. He stared across the kitchen, at the magnetized pad of paper on the front of the fridge. The words written there in Char's careful penmanship blurred as that day in the desert flooded his mind. "I lost everything below the knee, and it happened a little over four years ago. My third stint over in Iraq. I was on a truck at the end of a convoy that was hit by a bazooka rocket. We were acting as support for the local militia when we were ambushed."

"Did it hurt?" Steph shook her head and, folding her arms, looked down at the floor. "I'm sorry. That's a stupid question. I can't stop picturing you on that truck. The rocket exploding. You being hurled from the vehicle..." Her voice cracked, and she sniffled.

The knots in his gut finally eased. At least it wasn't the leg that bothered her.

He turned toward her, reaching up to wipe the tear from her cheek. He'd always hated when she cried. Being a strong, independent woman, she didn't do it often, and it wrenched at his gut every time.

"Oddly enough, it didn't hurt at first. It's how I knew something was wrong. I couldn't feel my leg. Hurt like a bitch when I came to in the hospital, though. It was a lot of physical therapy and learning how to walk again. Now..." He shrugged. "I'm used to it. It's just another part of me, I guess."

"But you were nervous to tell me." She offered an apologetic frown. "I'm sorry I got so upset. It wasn't the leg. It was just...shock, I guess. I'm still picturing you running circles around me and teasing me for being so slow."

"I can still run circles around you." He winked.

Steph rewarded him with a watery laugh.

"You're not the first person I've told, but it's never easy to do. I never know how people will react. Some people can't handle it."

She slipped her hand into his and squeezed his fingers.

"I am sorry. I should have stopped to think about how that would seem to you."

"It's okay." He dragged a hand through his hair and pushed away from the counter, sights set on the fridge on the other side of the small space. Maybe a beer would settle his damn nerves. "I just wanted you to know, so you won't be surprised later. *If* this goes anywhere, you'll need to know what to expect."

Before he could move too far, Steph caught the end of his tie and tugged him back. She stared for several seconds, eyes reaching and searching, probing all those deep places, before laying a hand against his chest.

"It doesn't bother me, I promise. At least, not in that way. I just don't like the thought of you being hurt. So relax. And for the record? This only goes as far as you're comfortable with." She gave him a tender smile, then just as quickly rolled her eyes, tossing him a playful reprimand and turned to the box on the counter. "Now, that's enough of this serious stuff, huh? You're making my mascara run."

He opened his mouth to apologize for making her cry, to thank her for being so understanding. For...hell. Being her. She'd always been able to do that, pull stuff out of him. Something about her had always just relaxed him. It awed him to think she still had it.

Before he could say any of that, she plucked a truffle from the box and turned back to him, pressing the chocolate to his lips. "Open."

He obeyed her soft demand and let her put the truffle in his mouth, biting it in half. Smooth dark chocolate melted on his tongue, followed by the sweet, creamy richness of caramel, with a hint of salt. A quiet moan worked its way out, loosening his stiff muscles. "I have a weakness for chocolate, and these are easily the best I've ever had."

Steph smiled, eyes gleaming with triumph, and something in that look cemented his decision. He needed—wanted—to let go of his guilt and move on. He'd have to take this step eventually. He'd go nuts staying single forever. Besides, she was already here, and they wanted the same things. For this weekend, he'd let go of his grief and guilt and let himself get lost. In her. In wherever the hell this night led him. It didn't have to be any more complicated.

Stomach hardening with resolve, he turned to the box on the counter.

"My turn." He canvassed the goodies, his gaze landing on a cupcake stacked with a healthy dose of white, creamy icing. He'd chosen a vanilla cupcake with key-lime-pie-flavored frosting. If he remembered correctly, she loved key lime pie. "Close your eyes and open your mouth."

The corners of her mouth twitched, but she did as he asked. He was reaching into the box when he remembered his dirty hands. He could hear his mother now. *"Don't you touch my cookies until you wash those filthy hands."*

He did an about-face, moved to the sink and pushed on the faucet.

"What are you doing?" Steph's voice held a hint of suspicion.

He darted a glance back at her. "Forgot to wash my hands. Dirty bike and all that."

She blew out a breath, her shoulders slumping. "Thought perhaps you were going to play dirty."

Because he had once upon a time. At her place on a Friday night, cleaning up after their weekly dinner and a movie had led to a playful moment. She'd teased him about the haphazard way he cleaned the dishes, and he'd turned the sink sprayer on her.

He chuckled. "You didn't really think I'd spray you again, did you?"

She grinned this time. "I wouldn't put it past you. That's exactly something you've done eleven years ago. Twice at least."

Both times she'd squealed and giggled and vowed vengeance, then gotten it in spades. He'd loved hearing her laugh. They'd ended up tangled between the sheets afterward. That was what he'd always loved about her. When he was with her, he could simply let go of his serious nature and be silly if the moment struck.

"I have grown up, you know." He dried his hands on the towel hanging from the oven door handle, then moved back to her, surprised to see her eyes still shut. He settled once again between her thighs, scooped a bit of the creamy icing off the cupcake, and held his finger over her luscious full lips. "Open."

When her lips fell open, he set his fingertip and the icing inside. "Now suck."

The corners of her mouth twitched, and her eyes opened. Wickedness glinted in the depths as she closed her lips around his finger. Her warm, wet tongue stroked the underside, a deliberate tease no doubt, then wrapped around it. She sucked gently, providing the right amount of pressure, and visions of her snapped into his thoughts. Namely, her hot mouth wrapped around his cock.

It didn't help the ache in his jeans any that he had memories of her doing exactly that. Christ. She'd given him similar looks then, too, peeking up at him from beneath those long, golden lashes. Even back then, Steph always knew when she had him right where she wanted him.

"Key lime. One of my favorites." She slid his finger from her mouth with a pop of suction, impishness and heat flashing in her gorgeous eyes. Then she turned to the box on the counter and scooped a fingerful of icing. Instead of offering it to him, the way he'd done with her, she smeared it across his lips.

His breathing grew harsh and ragged as his gaze zeroed in on her mouth. He held his breath in anticipation of her next move.

Steph didn't hesitate, but leaned in and drew his bottom lip gently into her mouth. Unbelievable pleasure flooded every cell in his body. The image of her on her knees, sucking his cock, flooded right behind it. God. If she kept that up, he was going to come in his jeans.

He couldn't stop the quiet groan that slid out of him. Steph was phenomenal at oral sex. She knew the exact right pressure, the right speed. Now she had his hard-on threatening to bust through his zipper.

He reached down, adjusting himself to a more comfortable position. "You're killing me here, you know."

Wickedness sparked in her eyes, but flitted away just as quickly, to be replaced with a warm concern. "Stop thinking, Gabe. I'm yours for the weekend. We can take this as fast or as slow as you need. If you want to stop here, I'm okay with that. But you're here for the same reason I am, right? Isn't that what we decided over dinner? That we wanted to get lost for a while?"

He settled his hands on her hips, let himself enjoy the simplicity of being able to touch her. That's what he'd missed the most since Julia's death. The softness of a feminine form. The warmth of a body. The house had only two bedrooms, but it was too damn big. He and Char seemed to ramble around in the space. It felt... empty without Julia. An ironic feeling for sure considering how their marriage had begun. He'd fallen in love with his wife *after* they'd married.

To be here with Steph, though, of all people, had guilt caging his chest again. Some part of him still insisted he was cheating on his wife. But he had to allow himself this time with Steph, if only because he needed it. At least for this weekend, he wouldn't have to sleep alone.

"You sure you're okay with that?" Short term was all he had to offer her, but it seemed wrong.

She gave him a gentle smile. "Positive."

The anxiety squeezing at his chest eased. He stroked his hands upward, letting his thumbs sweep her inner thighs. "I'm glad it ended up being you, you know. My date, I mean."

As he stood there with her, the truth hit him hard. Out of all the women he could have ended up with tonight, he was glad he'd ended up with someone who knew him so well. Right or wrong, good or bad, she seemed okay with the fact that he was a little fucked up. A little broken. The knowledge eased the last of the knots in his stomach.

"Me too." She stroked her hand down his chest, studying him for a moment, then reached into the box for another treat. This one, a chocolate-covered raspberry, she set in her mouth and tipped her chin at him.

He pressed his lips to hers, biting the chocolate in half. As he drew the treat into his mouth, he flicked his tongue along her lower lip, then pulled back enough to chew and swallow. Heat flared in her gaze as she did the same. Then she leaned in again.

The kiss began as a soft brush of lips. Tasting. Testing the waters. Getting acclimated to each other again. Her mouth opened beneath his, a quiet, serrated breath leaving her. Steph leaned into him, her breasts pushing into his chest. Her hands slid up his shoulders, slender fingers delving into his hair as she tilted her head.

Her tongue swirled into his mouth and the ember in his belly became a full-body burn. He slid his hands to her ass and pulled her closer. The front placket of his jeans settled against her belly, and he groaned. God, it had been too long since he'd last had this pleasure. To taste. To touch. Steph's softness, her body warm and inviting, her lips supple and pliant. Like a dying man handed a glass of water, he drank her in, unable to get enough.

When he was gloriously lost in her, she pulled back. He tightened his hold on her hips.

"Don't stop." The words left his mouth on little more than a hoarse whisper as he bent his head to her neck, seeking out any available skin.

A quiet moan vibrated out of her, her fingers tightening on his shoulders. "Tell me what you want, Gabe."

You to keep saying my name. It reminds me I'm still alive.

"I want to bury myself inside you. I want to feel your

body wrap around me and your nails rake down my back." He nipped at her earlobe, then sucked it into his mouth. "That specific enough for you?"

When he pulled back, her gaze scanned his face. After a moment, she took his hand, led him around the breakfast bar and down the long hallway leading to the back of the house. Every step retightened the coil in his stomach. Making love to another woman in the bedroom he and Julia had shared caused the guilt to rise all over again.

Steph, however, stopped outside the doorway and looked up at him. Clearly she wanted permission to enter, which told him she understood what this moment meant for him. The knowledge relaxed the coil in his gut.

He lifted their joined hands, kissing the back of hers, then moved around her into the room. He stopped at the dresser first, laying Julia's picture facedown on the top, then pulled Steph to the end of the bed. By the time he took a seat, the nervous tremors had seeped into his limbs again.

Steph braced her hands on his shoulders, slid onto his lap, straddling his thighs, and sat back on his knees. "Nervous?"

He let out a quiet laugh. "As a goddamn virgin."

She slid her hands around the back of his neck, soft fingers caressing his skin, and leaned forward, turning her mouth to his ear. "Would you rather unwrap me . . . or watch me strip?"

He drew a shuddering breath. His cock throbbed. God bless her.

"I'd rather unwrap you." He hadn't touched a woman in far too long, and he ached to get his hands on her. He might only allow himself the weekend, but he intended to enjoy every second of his time with her.

She leaned back and rolled her hips, grinding against him. "Then I'm all yours." She leaned her mouth to his ear again. "Know what I missed most about you, Gabe?"

The soft caress of her warm breath on his ear had the attention of every inch of him. The mischievous glint in her eye when she pulled back said she knew it, too. His cock twitched in his jeans, fire erupting through his veins.

Two could play at that game. He skimmed his hands up her stomach and over her breasts, letting his palms graze her tightened nipples, then slid her jacket from her shoulders. It dropped behind her, catching on her forearms, and he caressed his fingertips down the backs of her arms. Steph had incredibly sensitive skin, and goose bumps popped up along her arms.

He leaned in and flicked his tongue over her earlobe. "What's that, sweetheart?"

As hoped, a shiver moved through her, and her breathing hitched. Never one to be outdone, however, Steph straightened her arms, letting her jacket fall to the floor. Then she reached between their bodies and palmed his erection, caressing and squeezing him through the denim. "I remember you have a beautiful cock."

He let out a quiet laugh. "Ten years ago that word from your mouth might have had me on my knees."

He slipped his hands beneath the hem of her halter top, pushing it up. She obliged him and lifted her arms, allowing him to pull the shirt off. Her black lace bra teased him with a view of her nipples, straining against the fabric.

"But I've grown up." He pulled down the cups, exposing her breasts and pushing them up and out. Mouth watering, he cupped them in his palms, enjoying their soft weight, and flicked his thumbs over the taut tips. "You'll have to try harder than that."

He bent his head to her right breast first, sucking the elongated tip into his mouth. Such beautiful breasts, enough to spill out of his hands, but deliciously high and perky, with large, prominent nipples he'd never been able to resist.

She let out a throaty moan, and her nails slid along his scalp, fingers curling, hands pulling him in tighter. "Gabe?"

"Yeah?" He flicked his tongue over her nipple, then moved to the other breast, repeating the torture.

"You win. Enough talk."

He lifted his head in time to watch her slide from his lap. Standing before him, she reached behind her and unclasped her bra, letting it fall to the floor. Then she moved to the button on her jeans and popped it free. She turned her back to him, wiggling her tight little ass as she shoved her jeans and panties to her ankles. Then she straightened again and stepped out of them, kicking them aside. She finally turned around, blond hair now falling in disarray over her face.

He dragged his gaze over her, following the line of her body. From her breasts, full and round, to the feminine swell of her hips and the curve of the strong muscles of her thighs. For a long moment he could only stare, and Steph, God bless her, let him look before sashaying her way toward him and climbing onto his lap.

"Your turn." She took a seat on his knees and reached for his tie. After undoing the knot, she slid the blue silk from around his neck and dropped it to the floor, then moved to the buttons on his shirt, undoing them one by one. After freeing the last button, she reached for his waist and tugged his shirt-tails from his jeans. Her hands settled against his skin, sliding up his chest.

A groan escaped him, and Gabe closed his eyes. She had the softest hands, like warm silk, and that one simple action sent a heady tremor through him as she slid his shirt from his shoulders.

When it drooped on his forearms, he opened his eyes, concentrating for a moment on undoing his cuffs and shrugging out of his shirt. Because he couldn't touch her until he freed himself, and he needed his hands on her like he needed to breathe.

Steph leaned forward, raining kisses over his chest and shoulders, before pressing one to his lips. Arms now free, he cupped her face in his palms and leaned into her. The kiss became a soft tangle of lips and tongues, and for a moment he gave himself over to it, allowed himself to enjoy that one simple pleasure.

When they parted again, her eyes had dropped to half-mast, filling with a tenderness that awed him. He remembered that about her, too. Her tender side. He needed it, desperately, and he hadn't a damn clue how to tell her how much it meant that she gave it so freely.

Before he could find the words, Steph dropped her gaze and reached for the button on his jeans. "These are next."

When her fingers closed around the button, panic caged his chest in a vise. His hand shot out, catching her wrist before she popped the button free. She lifted her gaze to his, eyes wide with surprise. His hands shook, his heart beginning an erratic hammer as the moment settled over him.

Telling her he'd lost his leg was one thing. Showing her his stump was something else entirely. He'd have to watch the expression travel across her face when she caught her first glimpse of it.

He swallowed past the anxious lump forming in his throat. "The prosthesis will have to come off. It's the only way to get the jeans off. Well, I suppose it's possible to take the shoe off, but the leg is designed to work with the shoe. I can't walk barefoot or my hips aren't level, and my crutches are on the other side of the bed, and——"

Steph pressed a finger to his mouth. "Relax. It's okay."

He released a pent-up breath, his face catching fire. "I'm sorry." He dropped his gaze, busied himself with stroking his hands up her smooth thighs. "I'm nervous. Nobody but Molly and Julia have ever..."

Not even the guys at the shop had seen his leg. Oh, they all knew, but seeing it was something else entirely. Julia had been too sick by the time he returned from the war to do much more than hold him while they slept.

Steph stared, and his stomach lurched. Pathetic. That's what he was. A pathetic shell of a man. He should have known he was no longer cut out for the world of romance and never would be again. He ought to be seducing her, but instead he was a giant bundle of nerves. Any second now she'd get up and get dressed, make an excuse about having something important to do, and he wouldn't blame her if she did.

He opened his mouth, ready to let her off the hook, when she cupped his chin in her palm and forced his gaze back to hers. "It's okay."

"That's really nice, Steph, and I know you mean it, but

thinking it and seeing it for the first time are two different things." He'd never forget Molly's and Julia's expressions, the grief and shock that traveled across their features the first time they'd seen him after he'd come home four years ago. Of course, he understood they'd worried more about how close they'd come to losing him, but it still hadn't been easy to watch.

Steph cupped his face in the warmth of her palms, thumbs caressing his cheeks. "Do you trust me, Gabe?"

That was easy, at least. "You wouldn't be here if I didn't. Were you anybody else, the date would've ended with dinner, and I would have gone home alone."

She stroked her palm down his cheek. "Then trust me with this."

CHAPTER FIVE

Gabe didn't immediately answer, and the vulnerability playing on his face made Steph's chest clench. Eleven years ago he was self-assured almost to the point of being cocky, though he'd always tempered it with a playful sense of humor. Now his heart was in his eyes. The thought of her seeing his leg clearly made him anxious. She could think of only one way to help him relax: show him by undressing him.

She brushed a kiss across his mouth, hoping to divest him of his apprehension. Gabe leaned into her, slanting his mouth over hers, gripped her hips and tugged her closer, pressing her tight against the bulge in his jeans. His tongue stroked inside, a slow, sensual slide that wrenched a quiet moan from her and had her leaning in to get more. He still had it. Gabe Donovan still made kissing a freakin' art form. Stroking softly with his tongue. Nibbling at the corner of her mouth.

By the time they parted, she was breathless and trembling all over again. God, what he did to her.

She leaned her forehead against his as she attempted to catch her breath. "I want you naked. Sooner rather than later, because this cock"—she rocked her hips, sliding the heat of her against his erection—"is mine for the weekend, and I intend to take full advantage of it."

One corner of his mouth hitched. "You always were insatiable."

She swallowed a wry laugh. She'd only been that way for him, and even then, only because she'd trusted him. Outside of Mandy and Lauren, trust didn't come easily. Growing up on her own had taught her that.

"Get naked with me." She stroked a hand down his cheek and leaned her mouth to his ear. "Get these pants off, and you'll discover how wet you've made me."

His lips parted and his eyelids drooped, the heat within them scorching. His breath ramped up a notch, and his gaze locked on hers. Slowly, he slid a warm palm over her right thigh, dipped between, and cupped her mound. One long finger slipped between her slick folds and buried deep.

Steph gasped at the sweet invasion, her eyes closing. His fingertips held calluses, no doubt from turning wrenches all day, and the conflicting sensations, warm versus rough, lit her clit up like a vibrator. Her thighs trembled, her need out of control. "God, Gabe..."

He stroked her slowly, sliding his finger in and out, then using some of her natural moisture to rub her engorged clit. He growled low in his throat. "You *are* wet."

She dropped her head back and gave her body over to him, let him ply her at will. He continued to stroke and circle while his other hand slid around her breast, thumb and forefinger pinching her nipple. He knew exactly how she liked it, and heat burst over her skin, pleasure erupting along her nerve endings. A hot little coil wound tighter and tighter within her.

She arched her hips into his hand, certain from the shift in his breath that he watched. No man understood more than Gabe how much it turned her on when someone watched her receive pleasure. How many orgasms had she had while he watched, cock in his fist?

In no time at all she was panting into his shoulder and riding his hand, her hips bucking against the delicious press of his fingers. There was something to be said about a lover who knew your body. He didn't fumble and guess, making her more and more frustrated. Gabe knew exactly where and how to touch her, how to work her body, because he'd done it a thousand times before. It awed her to see they still had that, and every nerve ending responded, sending her careening toward bliss at breakneck speed.

"Come on, baby." Gabe's hot breath grazed her ear, his lips moving against the sensitive lobe. "Come for me, Steph."

Those words and the desperate need in his tone were her final undoing. It had the same need curling through her and sent her hurtling over the edge. With a quiet moan, she came apart at the seams, every muscle tightening and loosening in a white-hot wave of pleasure. Not once did he stop or slow down. His fingers kept flicking and stroking and pinching, and Steph cried out, racked by the seemingly never-ending, luscious spasms.

When the waves finally dwindled, she collapsed, breathless and trembling, against his chest, body as limp and lifeless as a cooked noodle. "I can't believe you can still make me come like that."

No one else. In eleven years, no other man had ever made her come so hard she forgot everything but the pleasure.

He bent his head, soft lips skimming her neck, her shoulders. "You're still damn beautiful when you let yourself go, too."

Her chest clenched. She'd always hated when he said things like that. It used to fill her with hope. That one day he'd see *her*. That he'd tell her he loved her, too.

She'd have to watch herself with him. Too easily he could pull her in. He still grieved the loss of his wife. She couldn't begrudge him that. Hell, part of her envied him, that he'd found love. She wouldn't, however, give him power over her. Not again. This was about sex, no more, no less. She had to remember that.

She lifted her head, gave him her best sultry smile, and tugged open the button on his jeans. "Your turn. Take these off."

He sighed. "I suppose I've stalled long enough. You know it's not you, right?"

Once again, quiet vulnerability erupted in his eyes, and it landed its punch right in her heart. God, he really had been hurt.

"I know." She brushed a tender kiss across his lips and slid from his lap, then folded her arms and arched a brow. "Pants, Gabe. Off. Now, please."

He pushed to his feet, towering over her, and grinned. "You're a bossy little thing."

"That's right." She smiled as she gripped his zipper, letting her fingers brush his erection as she carefully tugged it down. "And I usually get my way."

Gabe let out a quiet groan and leaned down, capturing her mouth in a fierce kiss that left her breathless, then, just as quickly, pulled back. He shoved his jeans down his thighs and took a seat on the end of the bed. One eye continually flicked in her direction as he took his right leg out of his pants and pushed the other down past his knee. He pressed something on his ankle and eased his leg from the device. Then he rolled down a thick padded sleeve, on the end of which appeared to be a small rod of some sort. Perhaps what connected his leg to the prosthesis?

Gabe made a show of moving his pants and prosthesis off to the side before finally looking up at her. Shoulders rounded, those gorgeous hazel eyes filled with a palpable anxiety as he gave a helpless shrug. "So. This is me."

Steph looked at his leg for a moment. Her chest hurt. Not just clenched, but wanted to cave in. He could've died, and the world would be one hero short.

He stiffened on the bed, sitting straighter, and folded his hands together in his lap. "Please put me out of my misery and tell me what you're thinking."

Her cheeks heated. Here she was, staring at him like an idiot. She knelt at his feet and ran her hand over his leg, down to where it stopped several inches below his knee.

A shudder moved through him, and she jerked her hand back and glanced up. "I'm sorry. Did I hurt you?"

"No. Nobody's ever touched me there before. Well, except Molly and Julia." He waved a hand in the air and rolled his eyes. "And the doctors and nurses, but you know what I mean."

Ah. Now they were getting somewhere. Determination swelled inside of her. She needed to show him she meant it when she said his leg didn't bother her. So she leaned over and pressed a series of kisses, starting at the top of his knee and moving down to where his leg ended.

This time he groaned softly, a sound of relief and desire all rolled into one. His fingers dove into her hair. "Jesus, Steph. Only you could possibly make this erotic."

She flicked her gaze to his as she planted another kiss. "I told you. I don't like the thought of you being hurt, but having half a leg doesn't make you any less of a man."

His gaze danced over hers. "Not everyone can handle this sort of thing."

She shifted closer, laying her hands on the tops of his strong thighs. Gabe stared, eyes heavy-lidded and filled with a soft heat. His fingers sifted through her hair, stroking like someone he cared about, and the tiny action made her chest clench again. She had a sneaking suspicion making love to him wouldn't be like most of the men she'd dated over the last couple of years. This might be only for the weekend, but Gabe would never be just a one-night stand. He knew all her secrets and vulnerabilities, and the knowledge left her feeling open and exposed. Laid bare.

"You're still you." She rose to her feet, braced a hand on his chest, and pushed him flat. Then she straddled his body, her thighs hugging his hips, and leaned down, pressing her chest to his. "You're still one of the sexiest men I know."

He rolled his eyes, one corner of his mouth quirking upward. "Now you're just filling my head."

She brushed her mouth over his, once, twice, then

stopped, holding herself a hairbreadth from him. She needed to get honest with him, in a way she probably shouldn't, but she had a feeling he needed to hear it. Sunday morning she'd be gone anyway. For tonight she'd indulge him.

"No. I'm not. I had a big crush on you a long time ago." Okay, so it had been a lot more than a crush. She'd fallen in love with him. But he didn't need to know that, and she had no desire to spill all her secrets. What he needed now was a whole lot more simplistic, and she needed to keep some semblance of a boundary with him or she'd end up in the same place—in love with a man who couldn't give her his heart.

Hands braced against his chest, she pushed upright. Her heat settled over the bulge in his shorts, and Steph rocked against him.

"That hasn't changed much. You still make me wet, and your smile still makes my heart skip a beat. Your leg is just part of you. Now make love to me, because I need you."

He groaned, big hands caressing up her stomach and over the curves of her breasts. His thumbs flicked her tightened nipples. Then he sat upright and covered her mouth with his. This time he didn't rush in. Gabe was Gabe. He nibbled at her bottom lip and sucked it into his mouth. Tangled his lips with hers, tongue flicking out, mimicking the act of lovemaking.

He took her breath her away, and she all but melted in his lap. All the while his hands never stopped kneading and caressing her breasts, always with the lightest of touches. Her skin came alive, and she was pretty sure his shorts had grown damp where he'd pressed against her hot core, because she throbbed.

"Underwear, babe," he murmured against her skin as his mouth moved, soft lips now trailing across her jaw and down her neck. "We'll never get anywhere if I don't take them off. And I need the condom in the back pocket of my jeans."

She nodded and slid from his lap. He lay back, lifting his hips as he eased his shorts down, then sat upright and pushed them down his legs. They fell to the floor and he dropped his hands to the bed, letting her look.

God, he was beautiful. Well-muscled shoulders and a wide chest tapered to a narrow waist, flat stomach, and lean hips. Small scars that hadn't been there eleven years ago littered his torso and the tops of his thighs. Shrapnel, she assumed. His chest and shoulders were thicker as well, his biceps more rounded. His cock stood high and proud against his stomach, the tip grazing his belly button. Her mouth watered, her insides clenching in delicious anticipation.

Gabe bent, digging into the pocket of his jeans and coming out with a foil packet. He tore it open, his gaze on hers and full of a searing hunger as he rolled the latex in place. Then he held out a hand. "You'll have to come a little closer."

She took his hand, letting him pull her to him, and climbed onto his lap. With her chest pressed against his and her knees on either of side his hips, she teetered on the edge of the bed, winding her arms around his shoulders for support. Taking every breath with him, she held herself over him, the tip of him pressing at her entrance. The anticipation had her thighs shaking already.

He caressed the curve of her backside, amusement glinting in his eyes. "Ride me, baby."

A hot little tremor raked the length of her spine, settling

in her core. The desire in his voice, the demanding request, all letting her know he understood what turned her on, had her core moistening further.

She threaded her fingers in his hair and slowly sank onto him, taking him inch by luscious inch. All the while, she kept her gaze on his, let his beautiful eyes take her world and spin it out of control.

When he was fully seated, his grip tightened on her ass, halting her movement, and his eyes fluttered closed.

"Stop moving." He dropped his head back on a long, quiet moan, mouth falling open in a look of utter bliss. "God, just for a minute."

She dropped her forehead to his shoulder, thighs shaking, core throbbing, and rocked her head back and forth. "You're killing me, Gabe. Please. I need to move."

It was torture not to rise and sink and satiate the hunger he sent burning through her like wildfire.

"Sorry. You just feel so good. So tight and slippery. It's been so damn long." He bent his head, his hot breath and soft lips a contrast of sensations as they skimmed her bare shoulder. His hands released her ass, his body trembling as hard as hers. "Go, baby. Take your pleasure."

A quiet, relieved groan tore out of her. Steph rose on her knees and sank, then rose and sank again, taking every inch of him with greedy abandon. His cock rubbed all those perfect places inside, and each hard thrust set her aflame, sending her careening once again toward sweet oblivion.

Gabe groaned. His hands pulled her in to him, grinding her clit against his pelvis. His lips skimmed her neck, her shoulder, her jaw. His warm breaths blew harsh against her skin. She was surrounded by and immersed in him, and every thrust lit her up as if he'd struck a match.

She gave up any semblance of control, buried her face in his throat, inhaling the clean, masculine scent of him, and rocked against him in time with his movements. Until they were pushing and surging together in a desperate frenzy. The bed squeaked. Gabe panted in her ear, big hands working her ass, pulling her to him harder and faster.

Her climax struck out of nowhere. She cried out, bucking against him as luxurious, bone-melting pleasure tore through her.

Gabe dropped his head into her shoulder, a quiet curse leaving his mouth. He pulled her to him once, twice, then held her there, his grip on her ass so tight it was almost painful as his body shuddered against her. He moaned his satisfaction into her throat, long and low.

When the tremors ended, he collapsed back on the bed, taking her with him, and wrapped his arms tight around her. His chest rumbled beneath her, his body shaking with his quiet, breathless laugh. "Jesus. I'd forgotten how intense it was making love to you."

Steph continued to tremble as an ultra-vulnerable sensation curled through her, and she snuggled into his neck, needing his strength, his solidity. "It's still there."

He still had the power to make her see stars, and like eleven years ago, he'd never see her as anything more than great sex. It was bliss and torture all rolled into one and so damn familiar. Gabe was the only man, outside of Alec, to ever get past her defenses. And then he'd left, walked out of her life like she'd meant nothing to him. Eleven years might have passed, but clearly her heart hadn't forgotten that part. Not that she could ever regret this moment.

Gabe went silent. She ached to know what he was thinking but couldn't bring herself to ask. It was better this way, to keep a firm distance between them.

Finally, he lifted his head and pressed a kiss to her shoulder. "Thanks."

She let out a quiet laugh. "Gabe Donovan, if you're thanking me for great sex I'm going to hit you."

She meant her words as a tease, but he didn't laugh. Instead, he caressed her back, fingertips walking her skin. "Not for the sex. For having patience with me."

God, there he went again, melting her heart right out from beneath her with a few simple words. She wrapped her arms tight around his body and pressed a kiss to his damp neck. "You're worth it."

She meant that. Far more than she ought to.

CHAPTER SIX

They lay in the dark an hour later, Steph tucked against his side, her head on his shoulder. Gabe had closed his eyes a dozen times, but sleep refused to come. Steph's fingers kept trailing over his chest and belly, a sign she hadn't fallen asleep either, yet neither of them had said anything for quite some time.

For a few blissful moments, she'd made him forget the pain of losing Julia, and for the first time in too long, he wasn't lying alone staring at the damn dark ceiling. But Steph had gone a little too quiet. Eleven years ago, they'd lain together in the dark and talked. About upcoming schedules, exams, frustrations. This was the space where they were always the most vulnerable with each other.

The silence gave him too much time to think. He'd loved Julia, as much as a man could love a woman, yet she hadn't made him feel quite like this. Steph's body against his side was as comfortable as a favorite pair of sweats and as natural as breathing. The realization had guilt caging his chest again.

He turned his head, kissing Steph's forehead. "I know you're awake. Talk to me. I'm going nuts over here."

Steph looked up at him, her hand stilling over his heart. "Sorry. I thought you'd be asleep by now."

He made a sound of acknowledgment at the back of his throat. "I don't sleep most nights."

She tucked her forehead into the curve of his neck, her voice taking on that sleepy, lovers-in-the-dark quality he knew too well. "The war?"

"Sometimes. Mostly...I just hate being alone." He stroked his hand down her back, following the curves and dips of her body, letting the warmth and solidness of her soothe the ache in his chest. "Is it always like this? So awkward, I mean?"

One-night stands really weren't his style. They might have been once, but life with Char and Julia had changed him. These days, he was an old-fashioned kind of guy. One woman for the rest of his life had suited him fine. Except she was gone, and here he was, back in the dating pool again. Never mind that he hadn't done casual since...well, Steph.

"It depends." Her shoulder hitched as she sifted her fingers through the hair on his chest. "Tell me about your wife. How did you meet?"

He drew a deep breath and released it. The thought of explaining this to her had another band of guilt closing around him. The urge to talk to her, the way he used to, pulled at him all the same. Maybe if he got it out, talking would soothe the awkwardness between them. "Julia and I met when I went home to settle my parents' estate. Molly stayed at a friend's house one night, and I went to a local bar to get so damn drunk I couldn't think anymore. Julia was bartending. At the end of the night, she cut me off and took me home. One thing led to another."

He reached up to rub his forehead. That night wasn't the proudest moment of his life. It was one big blur. Yet it had led to a friendship he'd treasured and had resulted in the greatest gift he could have ever received—Char. It had also started him down a path that had led him to where he was today, and he could never regret the direction his life had taken him. It was that weekend he'd decided to put off law school so Molly could finish her senior year at home with her friends. Life had changed on a dime, and his dreams of becoming a lawyer had shifted with it.

"About two months after we started seeing each other, she told me she was pregnant."

Steph stiffened against his side. "And you asked her to marry you."

He blew out a heavy breath. Leave it to her to know him so well, even eleven years later.

He closed his eyes, his gut churning. Looking back now, the way his marriage had begun sounded so…meaningless. "Because it was the right thing to do. It was the way my father taught me. I didn't want my child growing up torn between two parents. I'd had enough friends over the years with parents who could barely tolerate each other. I didn't want that."

He'd wanted Char to have what he'd had—love and security.

Steph's fingers stroked up his chest. She remained silent, but her unspoken thoughts hung heavy in the air between them. His gut knotted as he waited for the fallout. Did she hate him for the way he'd handled things back then? For jumping into another relationship so soon after her, for losing track of her over the years, like she'd meant nothing at all?

Finally, she shifted against his side, as if trying to get comfortable again. "That's very noble, but people make it work all the time."

He shrugged. "Maybe, but I didn't want to find out. We might not have planned to get pregnant, but she deserved someone to stand by her."

He'd refused to be just another person on the long list of people who'd abandoned her.

"It's partly what made me decide to enlist, actually. After she graduated, Molly got accepted at UCLA, and I wanted to move with her. She's the only family I have left. If she was moving, even if only for a few years, I was for damn sure going with her. Jules was six months pregnant by that time, so I asked her to marry me."

"She said yes," Steph murmured from his chest.

He grunted in acknowledgment. "I wanted to create a home for the three of them, Molly, Julia and the baby." He let out a quiet laugh, remembering that day. "Apparently I'd impressed her."

Steph tilted her head, peering up at him. "What made you decide to enlist rather than go back to school?"

He shrugged. "Dad. He'd served, and I wanted to make him proud. And, with a baby on the way, I was going to need a job. Just felt...right."

Steph patted his chest. "You're a decent guy, Gabe."

"I'm not sorry I married her, though. It was comfortable,

and Char was happy. After I enlisted, Julia kept an eye on Molly for me. She was always home base."

His only regret for the direction his life had taken him was that Steph had been a casualty.

Steph's hand stilled on his chest. "Were *you* happy, though?"

He swallowed a wry laugh. She didn't miss anything. No doubt that instinct made her an excellent lawyer. "It wasn't all candy and roses. We lived like strangers for a while, and we argued a lot in the beginning. About every damn little thing. With the SEALs, I was gone all the time, and for a while sex was...nonexistent.

"Wasn't long after I got out that we discovered Julia had a brain tumor. It's how we ended up in Seattle. One of the top cancer treatment hospitals in the country is here. I was a miserable son a bitch back then, feeling sorry for myself. She was my rock. I wanted her to have the best."

He caught his last words as they left his mouth on a hoarse whisper. His stomach knotted. Shit. He hadn't meant to tell her all that.

"I'm sorry. That was probably more than you wanted to know."

In the darkness he couldn't see her eyes, but she tilted her head up. She remained silent a moment, as though studying him, then slid her palm over his pecs. "It's hard being here with me. It's why you turned the picture over."

He made a sound of agreement at the back of his throat, opened his mouth to apologize—again—when she pressed a finger to his lips.

"Don't apologize. I'm sorry I said I didn't want to talk

about your family at first. Seeing you is kind of throwing me for a loop. I panicked and resorted to rules I used to abide by in my relationships. That was one of them. I didn't want to talk."

That wasn't the first time she'd hinted being with him wasn't easy for her, the fact of which brought up a thousand questions. "Why didn't you ever tell me you felt that way about me? That you wanted more than just the sex. That's what you meant, isn't it, when you said you had a crush?"

She let out a quiet, breathless laugh. "Of all the questions for you to ask. Would it have changed anything?"

He sighed. He hated telling her this, too, but he had to be honest. "No. Probably not."

Eleven years ago he'd been a different man. He'd been too wrapped up in himself, in where he wanted to go in life, to worry about things like relationships. It wasn't until Steph was no longer in his life that he'd begun to appreciate her place in it.

Steph lifted out of the space beside him, sliding over the top of him, and lay along his length, forearms braced against his chest. Her hair created a curtain around his head, and the soft perfume of her shampoo filled his lungs with every breath. "Then it doesn't matter now."

He settled his hands on her back. "I'm sorry."

"For what?" The tip of her index finger traced his lower lip, her voice coming soft and thoughtful, as if she'd gotten lost in her thoughts.

"That we drifted apart. You deserved better. I didn't know what to tell Julia about you and me. It wasn't usual what we had, and I didn't want to give her anything that would make her doubt me. For a while our relationship was so...fragile. So I just didn't tell her." The heat of shame flooded his face. God, the words sounded so lame when he said them out loud. They sounded like little more than a careless excuse. Did she think he was an ass? He sure as hell felt like one. "And then time moved on and life got busy, and—"

Her mouth settled over his, her kiss soft, luxurious, slow. She kissed him until he couldn't think about anything but the slight weight of her body and her tongue swirling into his mouth. In seconds he hardened, his cock stretching up his belly and reaching for her.

Finally, she pulled back, and although her face was little more than a play of shadows, he could swear she smiled at him. "Gabe?"

The husky tone of her voice called to him like a beacon in the dark. He stroked his hands down her back, settling them over the luscious curves of her ass. God, she had the finest ass, taut and round. "Yeah?"

"Stop apologizing." She nipped at his bottom lip, hard enough to hurt, then soothed the bite with a soft stroke of her tongue and rocked her hips into his now straining erection. "Condom."

Heart hammering, Gabe nodded in the direction of the bedside table. "Nightstand."

She flicked her tongue along his bottom lip, then stretched to reach into the top drawer. After pulling out a condom and rolling it down his length, she straddled him again. She sat there a moment, the tip of him pressed at her entrance, then, with a roll of her hips, sank onto him, taking him to the hilt in one long, slow thrust. Pleasure shot to his toes, and Gabe groaned, tightening his grip on her ass cheeks.

Steph didn't give him time to think or even to react. She sat up, hands braced on his chest, and rode him hard, rising and sinking with abandon. Until he couldn't think at all. At least, not about anything but her. She was little more than an erotic play of shadows, all curves and movement, but he was lost in what he *could* see. Her mouthwatering breasts bounced with every thrust. Her head dropped forward, soft hair falling to tease his skin every time she moved. Her breaths soughed in and out of her mouth, and she let out a litany of needy moans, each one more desperate than the last.

She took her pleasure on his cock, using his body like she owned him, and it set his blood on fire. Every hard thrust jarred through him.

He slid his hands up her taut stomach and around her breasts, thumbing her nipples. "You are so fucking beautiful, you know that?"

In no time at all, she had him shaking, panting along with her, and on the edge of release. He gritted his teeth until his jaw ached, trying desperately to hold on to himself, and slid one hand between their bodies. When he went, for damn sure he was taking her with him.

"Let it go, Steph." He found her swollen clit and massaged it slowly. "Come on, baby. Come with me."

She let out a moan that sounded torn from her chest. Her thighs began to shake, and her body rhythmically squeezed his cock, telling him she was close. He worked her clit faster, flicking it back and forth with his thumb.

Seconds, minutes later, she stiffened above him and cried

out, her body clamping around him, and began to shudder. Her inner walls squeezed him, and his own orgasm slammed into him. His fingers dug into her ass cheek, her name leaving his lips on a hoarse groan as she took his world and spun it wildly out of control.

When the spasms finally ended, she collapsed on his chest, her body warm and heavy. Her harsh breaths puffed against his throat. Steph purred, the sound of a contented cat after a bowl full of cream. One hundred percent pleased with herself.

"You're amazing, you know that?" He wrapped his arms around her back and turned his head to kiss her shoulder. "You're exactly what I needed."

She slid off to his side, laying her head in the crook of his arm. "Ditto. But if you say thank you again, I really am going to hit you."

He let out a breathless laugh.

* * *

"Dad?"

Char's voice jerked him from a dead sleep. Gabe groaned, rubbed his eyes, and pulled himself upright. "I'm up. I'm up."

His foot hit the floor and he finally pried his heavy lids open, his gaze landing on the blazing red numbers of the digital alarm clock. Soft, steady breathing sounded behind him, and he swiveled his head, peering at the bed behind him. Steph lay on her stomach, covered only by the sheet and comforter, eyes closed, mouth slack in slumber.

He darted a glance at the bedroom door. Indistinguishable

conversation drifted down the hallway, and he furrowed his brow. Wait a minute... What the hell day was it?

Reality slammed into him. Sunday. It was Sunday, and Molly had apparently brought Char home early. Steph was supposed to be out before they got home.

His heart took off on a sprint, hammering his rib cage. Shit.

He leaned back on an elbow, brushing the hair off Steph's face, for a moment caught by the sight of her. He'd had her to himself for the entire weekend. Saturday had seemed like old times, spent laughing and talking and making love, another day and night together solidifying how comfortable they were with each other.

He hated seeing his time with her end.

"Steph... baby, wake up." He pressed a kiss to her cheek, then sat up again and reached for his pants and leg. As he shoved his legs into his pants, he scrambled to come up with a reason for Char not to come in here, settled on one, then called out to her, "Char, stay in the living room. I'm not dressed. I... spilled coffee on my pants. Where's Aunt Molly?"

It was flimsy damn excuse, but if she came in here, she'd find Steph in his bed. Thank God she hadn't come into the room to wake him the way she sometimes did.

"Here." Molly's voice drifted down the hallway just as he was rolling the liner onto his stump. "I'm sorry we're early. Char's excited. She wants to know how your date went Friday night."

That Char wanted details about his date was a good thing. It meant that, so far, she really had accepted his dating again.

While she played brave and supportive, watching him go out with someone else couldn't be easy. Her timing, however, couldn't have been worse.

He let out a quiet groan as he slid his leg into the prosthesis, then stood, listening for the clicks as his stump settled securely into the socket. Just his freakin' luck. Most weekends, Molly brought Char home late, sometimes not showing up until noon. They enjoyed their time together. Char loved having a woman to do things with, and three "sisters." Today of all days she had to want to come home early?

After getting himself fully situated, he pulled up his jeans and darted a backward glance at the bed as he buttoned and zipped them. Steph, of course, hadn't so much as moved an inch. Mouth slack, her hair fanning the pillow behind her, she looked peaceful and beautiful. He hadn't seen that particular sight in eleven years. He almost hated to wake her. Almost.

Heart in his throat, he darted a glance at the door and called out to Molly and Char, "I'll be out in a minute. Don't go anywhere, Moll. I need to talk to you."

"Okay..."

He shoved his foot into his other shoe and sat down to tie it, then leaned back on the bed. This time he dragged the tips of his fingers down the back of Steph's arm and leaned his mouth beside her ear. "Wake up, sleepyhead."

She let out a sleepy moan, and his heart launched itself into his throat.

He pressed a finger to her lips. "Shhh. Get up, babe. Char's home."

Steph frowned in her sleep. "Who's Char?"

He rolled his eyes. Steph could sleep through a tornado.

He leaned his mouth to her ear and tried again. "My daughter. You know, the cute ten-year-old I live with? Keep your voice down. She doesn't know you're here."

Steph's eyes popped open. She blinked for a moment, then rolled onto her back and pulled the covers up over her bare chest. "Shit."

"Yeah, shit. Get dressed but stay here. I'll see if I can get rid of them."

Steph shook her head, eyes widening now with panic. "They have to know *someone's* here, Gabe. My car's in the driveway."

He halted midstride halfway to the bedroom door and wiped a hand down his face. "Son of a *bitch*."

How the hell did he get himself out of this one?

Already on her feet, Steph plucked her panties off the floor and stepped into them. "I came over for breakfast and spilled coffee on my shirt."

He dropped his arms, shoulders rounding. The whole prospect of sneaking around just exhausted him. He turned sideways to face her and flung a hand in the air in frustration.

"But I'm in here with you. Supposedly changing my pants." He let out a heavy sigh. "Stay here. I'll figure something out."

He closed the bedroom door behind him, then strode down the hallway. As he emerged into the living room, Char came into view. She sat on the couch, gaze glued to the cartoons on the TV. Their playful noise filled the air, easing the knots in his chest a fraction. Good. Maybe she hadn't heard Steph after all.

He turned his head. Molly was in her usual place whenever

she came over—in his kitchen. She currently appeared to be setting up the coffeepot. As he rounded the breakfast bar, she darted a glance over her shoulder. "Morning, sunshine."

He shot her an irritated frown as he crossed the space to her, keeping his voice low enough only she would hear him. "I thought you said you'd call before you came over."

Molly studied him for a moment, then let out a quiet laugh and closed the lid on the coffeemaker. She stabbed the ON button and turned to lean back against the counter. "How was I supposed to know you'd actually bring your date home or that you'd keep her here for more than one night? I take it by this cold coffeepot that she's still here?"

He dragged a hand through his hair, his stomach lurching.

Molly shot him a mischievous grin and nudged him with an elbow. "Go you."

"Ha ha." He inclined his head in the direction of the living room. "What the hell do I tell her?"

The coffee began to drip into the pot, filling the kitchen with the aroma of the fresh brew. His stomach rumbled, and Molly turned to the cabinet over the coffeemaker, pulled open the left side, and got down two mugs. "You could just be honest with her."

He let out a harsh laugh. "Dad had a sleepover. Yeah, 'cause that's a conversation I want to have with my ten-year-old."

Molly pursed her lips and shook her head, pulled out the sugar bowl and lifted the lid to check the contents. Then she bent into a low cabinet. "It's a conversation you're going to have to have with her sooner or later if you really want to start dating, Gabe. She's ten, and she's in advanced classes at school. She *will* figure it out eventually. For now I'll take her to the bakery to pick out something for breakfast."

"I'm not sure I *want* to do this again." He dragged his hands through his hair, holding his bangs back off his forehead. "Christ. I'm not sure my heart can take it."

Molly let out an entirely too-pleased-with-herself laugh as she refilled the sugar bowl. "Just wait till *she* starts dating."

He shot her a sideways glare. "Not even remotely funny. She can't date until she's thirty."

"Yeah, you keep telling yourself that, Dad." Molly clapped him on the back as she moved around him, heading out of the kitchen. As she rounded the breakfast bar, she called out to Char, "Hey, sweetie. Dad's all out of eggs. How about we go get him some of those muffins he likes, from that bakery down the street?"

"Okay." Char turned her gaze from the television to Molly and nodded. As she and Molly made their way to the front door, Char glanced out the front window. "Whose car is that in the driveway?"

Gabe's stomach flipped. Panic set his heart hammering in his ears. He didn't have a fucking clue how to answer that.

Molly wrapped an arm around Char's shoulder and leaned down, a conspiratorial tone to her voice as she guided them toward the front door. "His date. They must have had so much fun Friday night, he invited her over for breakfast. But Dad forgot to buy eggs. So we'd better save him and go get him some of those muffins."

Gabe rolled his eyes. Of course Molly would invite Steph to stay for breakfast. No doubt she wanted to check out his date.

Char shook her head as they stepped outside. "He never 'members to go shopping."

The door shut behind them, closing off the rest of their conversation. Gabe sagged back against the counter and blew out a breath, dragging a hand down his face. Jesus. He wasn't cut out for this sneaking around crap. Now came the hard part: he had to tell Steph.

He pushed away from the counter and made his way to the bedroom. Inside, Steph sat on the end of the bed, fully dressed. Her back was ramrod straight, and she had her hands folded in her lap, but anxiety danced in her eyes as she looked up at him.

He stopped in front of her, reaching up to rub the back of his neck. "I'm afraid I have good news and bad news."

She blinked. "Okay...."

"They're gone. For now."

She lifted a brow. "Why do I hear a *but* in there?"

He plastered on the brightest smile he could muster. God, here went nothing. "You're supposedly here for breakfast, but I forgot the eggs. They're going down to the bakery to get some muffins, which means they'll be back."

"And they're expecting me to stay." Steph sat staring at him, but her eyes glazed over.

As he waited for her reaction, his gut clenched in anticipation. He couldn't be sure if he wanted her to tell him she'd stay... or that she had to leave. When regret rose in her eyes, however, disappointment sank in his stomach. She didn't want to stay.

"Sorry. I know this isn't what we agreed on, but Char's ten. We couldn't exactly tell her the truth." He stuffed his hands in his pockets and gave a helpless shrug. "I wasn't expecting them to come back so early."

Steph leaned forward, braced her elbows on her knees, and ducked her head into her hands. "I'm not good with kids. I work with divorcing couples. You know, things like who gets the house?"

"Then don't worry about it. I'll tell them you had a family emergency. I'm sorry they put you in this position." Heart in his sneakers, he turned, intending to head back into the kitchen.

"Gabe . . ."

He stopped at the bedroom doorway but couldn't bring himself to turn around. What the hell could he tell her? Admit it disappointed him that she didn't want to stay and he hadn't a fucking clue why? What good would that do, except make her more uncomfortable than she already was?

The bed creaked, and her quiet footsteps came up behind him. When he forced himself to face her, she settled a hand against his chest, her shrewd gaze working his face. "You're disappointed."

Damn. Clearly he was still transparent to her. "Yes, I'm disappointed. We didn't get to have breakfast before you left. It kind of feels like I'm kicking you out, and that just sits wrong with me. I meant it when I said I don't know how to do this. Don't worry about it. I'll figure it out. I always do."

He pushed away from the doorway, calling to her as he headed for the kitchen.

"You should go. They'll be back soon, and I can guarantee Molly's going to give you the third degree."

He was halfway through pouring himself a cup of coffee

when Steph leaned against the counter beside him. She gripped the edge behind her and looked over at him. "It's been eleven years, but you still get the same look on your face when something's bugging you. Want to talk about it?"

He let out a harsh laugh and sipped at his coffee. It burned a path down his throat, but the dose of caffeine gave his brain the jolt he needed. "No."

"Come on, big guy. Talk to me." She leaned sideways, bumping his shoulder.

He heaved a sigh and gave in, because his gut was tied in knots, and Steph was...Steph. Damned if he could resist the lure of her. His marriage to Julia had worked in large part because they'd allowed each other a measure of privacy, the space to be individuals. They'd only fallen in love there at the end. Her getting sick had brought them together. Yet for all of its challenges, their relationship had worked.

Steph had always left him feeling open and raw. Vulnerable. She was addicting and terrifying.

"This just became a whole lot more complicated than I anticipated. My daughter now knows you were here, and she's going to have questions I haven't a clue how to answer. This whole parenting thing doesn't come with a fucking handbook."

He pushed off the counter and straightened, staring out the window at the gray clouds blanketing the sky. Julia had always handled shit like this. She'd also left him alone with his private thoughts, never tried to pull them out of him the way Steph always managed to do.

Steph came up behind him, placed a gentle hand on his shoulder, lessening his irritation.

"We probably should have just gone to your place, but you made me laugh, and I forgot myself." He shook his head, disgusted with himself, and sipped at his coffee. "I wasn't thinking much past getting lost in you."

And he had. Too much so.

Steph remained silent a moment, but her thoughts filled the space between them. He couldn't be sure whether or not he wanted her to voice them.

"I'll stay."

Surprised by the soft agreement, Gabe glanced back. Steph had turned to the coffeemaker and was pouring the steaming liquid into one of the mugs Molly had gotten down. Like it was any other morning. Like their cozy weekend hadn't just imploded. Hadn't she just told him she wasn't good with kids? He'd gotten the clear impression she didn't want to stay. So what changed her mind?

Deciding he had to know, he turned to face her. "Why would you do that?"

She turned, glancing at him over the rim of her mug as she took a sip, eyes dancing with playful impishness. "Just so happens I don't actually have anywhere to be this morning."

He turned back to the window. He knew a line when he heard one, but if she didn't want to tell him the truth, he wouldn't push her. "Thanks, but you don't have to do that."

She released a long, heavy breath, the sound one of defeat and acceptance. "All right. You want the truth?"

He tossed a smile over his shoulder. "That might be nice."

One corner of her mouth quirked upward, recognition and amusement lighting in her eyes. It didn't escape his notice that her mug trembled as she lifted it to take a sip, though.

Or that she turned to gaze in the direction of the living room instead of looking at him.

"You could have shut me out, but you didn't. Honestly, I didn't expect you to be so straightforward with me, except you've been nothing but since we met in the park Friday night. Truth is, I needed this weekend. All of it. I'm grateful to you for that. You sound overwhelmed." She shrugged, a soft pink rising in her cheeks. "I'd like to help."

Gabe could only stare for a moment. Once again, she was that vulnerable woman who pulled at all those deep places inside of him. That woman scared the hell out of him. Being with her was so damn easy. She simply accepted him at face value.

He set his coffee mug on the breakfast bar and crossed to her, cupped her cheeks in his palms, and tilted her face to his. She stared at him, eyes liquid and tender and so goddamn vulnerable. "I needed that, too. More than I can tell you. But I can't ask you do this."

"You're not. I'm offering. Clearly the thought of facing her is eating at you, and to be honest, I hate that it does." She settled her hands on his pecs, her skin warm and soft. "Let me help."

"I owe you." Too damned stunned by her generosity, he leaned down, brushing his mouth over hers, then released her. "I need to go put a shirt on. They should be back soon."

CHAPTER SEVEN

Two days with him, and she was already in over her head.

Steph's gut clenched as Gabe disappeared around a bend in the hallway. She'd gone and extended their time together. As he'd left the bedroom, he'd gotten that all-too-familiar look on his face. Gabe had always tended to bottle his emotions, and like the last eleven years hadn't happened, she'd done what she always used to—offered to help. Clearly she hadn't learned her lesson at all. A weekend fling with a nice guy she could handle. Not to mention it had been a chance to do what she'd spent eleven years wishing for—to reconnect with him. If only for a few days.

It was supposed to be just a damn weekend. Yet here she was, volunteering to stay for breakfast with his daughter. What could she do, though? Leaving him to deal with the aftermath by himself seemed cruel.

The low rumble of a car engine drifted in from outside, and her heart launched itself into her throat. She hadn't a damn clue how to relate to a ten-year-old.

Stomach tied in sickening knots, she moved around the breakfast bar and took a seat. She willed her hands to stop shaking and sipped at her coffee, hoping the dose of much-needed caffeine would bolster her nerves.

Gabe came up the hallway then, tugging down a navy T-shirt as he moved. As he came to a stop at her side, she set her coffee on the counter and pulled a hand through her hair. "Do I look like I just rolled out of bed?"

The right corner of his mouth quirked upward, those hazel eyes dancing at her. "You do have a 'thoroughly fucked' look about you."

"That helps. Thanks." She rolled her eyes, but his teasing eased the knots in her stomach. Only by a fraction, but she'd take it. "How is it you're not coming out of your skin?"

"Because as I was dressing I reminded myself that she's my daughter. I see her every day. That's what I'm choosing to focus on." He moved around the breakfast bar and picked up his own coffee, peering at her over the rim. "Relax. She isn't going to notice or care whether or not you're perfectly put together. All she's going to care about right now is that Dad has a breakfast date."

Steph gave a bitter laugh. "Again, that doesn't help."

The front door opened and then closed again with a quiet snap. Steph's whole body tensed until her shoulders ached. She sat straighter on her stool and clutched her coffee mug to root her. God. Here went nothing. The performance of a lifetime.

Plaster on a smile and pretend it's your best day. It's how she got through everything.

Gabe came around the center island and slid onto the stool

beside her. He bumped her shoulder with his, his voice meant only for her. "Relax."

Her mug trembled as she lifted it to her mouth. "I'm not sure that's possible."

A thin redheaded girl and a short brunette emerged into the main room of the house. The girl stopped at Gabe's side, peering at Steph with wide, curious eyes. The woman moved around the breakfast bar and into the kitchen.

A broad grin slid across Molly's face as she set a white bakery box on the counter. "I'm so glad to meet the woman who finally got my hermit of a brother out of the house."

Steph had only seen pictures of Molly before, back when she'd known Gabe in college. Molly had been a teenager then, but there was no mistaking the familial resemblance. She had the same greenish-brown eyes and dark curls Gabe had.

Steph moved to slide from the stool, but Molly shook her head and held out a hand. "No need to get up. I'm Molly, Gabe's sister."

Steph shook Molly's hand, plastering on a smile she prayed wasn't wobbling. "Steph. Nice to meet you."

The girl had yet to say anything, only stared. Steph squirmed inside but did her best not to show it. Gabe was a father. God, the word seemed so foreign to her. Nothing demonstrated how much he'd changed as this moment right here.

Gabe swiveled sideways and turned to hook an arm around the girl. Steph suddenly felt like a third wheel and completely out of place. A stranger in a strange land. A cold sweat moved across her skin, and she clutched her shaking hands on her thighs.

Gabe gave the girl a soft smile. "You chatter at me all morning, every morning. Now suddenly the cat's got your tongue?" When she gave him a shy little shrug, he rubbed the girl's back and turned to Steph. "This is Char."

Steph's stomach roiled so hard she was afraid she'd puke. Taking a deep breath, she drew up the image of her office at work, pulled the power of her profession around her like a shield, and stuck out her hand. If she could deal with cranky judges and cocky attorneys, she could talk to a ten-year-old.

"Nice to meet you. I have to say, you don't look anything like your father." She let her gaze roam the girl's face. "Well, except maybe the eyes. Those are definitely Gabe's eyes."

Char blinked for a moment, then slipped her hand into Steph's, shaking it like she'd done it a thousand times before. Despite the girl's clear nervousness, she had a sure, strong grip. "I look like my mom. She had red hair, too."

As she pulled her hand back, Steph picked up the easy conversation thread. Thinking of Char like a client calmed her nerves a bit. She made conversation with people all the time. "Your mom must have been very pretty."

Char dropped her hand, seemed to study her for a moment, darted a glance at Gabe, then drew a breath. "Yeah. She died."

Gabe casually turned his stool to face the breakfast bar, where he picked up his mug. His acute awareness prickled in the air around them. Even Molly, who, up until this point, had busied herself with getting out plates and napkins, seemed to still.

Steph drew her shoulders back and focused on the sad acceptance hanging on the girl. Here, at least, they had something in common. She gave the girl a sympathetic frown. "Your dad told me. I'm so sorry. You must miss her very much."

Char gave a sad little nod. "Yeah. She had a tumor. But Aunt Molly says she's in heaven now, so she's all better."

"You know, I lost my mom when I was about your age. She was sick, too. For a really long time. I'm sure your aunt Molly's right, but I still miss my mom like crazy."

"Yeah." Char let out a heavy sigh, then just as suddenly brightened a bit. Her brows rose, hope filling her eyes. "Aunt Molly and me went to the bakery. We got muffins and bagels. 'Cause Dad forgot the eggs." She pursed her lips and gave a stern shake of her head, sending her curls bouncing. "He never 'members to go shopping."

"Sorry, sweetheart, but I'm a terrible cook. I think we both know you're better off eating with Aunt Molly." Gabe darted a glance at Steph and shrugged. "Julia always did that stuff."

"No, you're not. You make the best spaghetti." Char looked to Steph again. "Do you want a bagel? They're my favorite."

Steph bit the inside of her cheek to keep from giggling as she watched the exchange. Molly, she noted, seemed to be doing the same. Gabe would have his hands full with this one when she was a teenager. She already had her father on a string.

Steph smiled and nodded. "A bagel would be lovely, thank you. Just so happens they're *my* favorite, too."

Char flashed a thousand-watt smile, eyes lit up and all but glowing, and skipped around the counter to lift the lid on the bakery box. "With lots of cream cheese, right?"

Steph swiveled her chair to face the counter and curled her hands around her coffee, grateful for the ease settling over the kitchen again. "Is there any other way?"

Char ducked into a low cabinet and pulled out an odd-looking device that resembled a guillotine. She set a bagel inside the holder, then pushed down the handle, slicing the bagel neatly in half without risk to her fingers.

Gabe set his elbows on the edge of the counter, his gaze on Molly, who seemed to busy herself with cleaning an already sparkling kitchen. "You know, Steph and I knew each other in college."

Molly's head perked up, surprise in her gaze as it darted between Steph and Gabe. "Really?"

Char pulled the bagel from the slicer and set it on a paper plate, gaze now intent on Steph. "What was he like?"

The memories filled her mind, of the first six months she'd known Gabe, and Steph let out a quiet laugh. "Your dad always had a gaggle of girls swooning over him. When we met, he was on the track team, a sprinter. You should have seen him when he crossed the finish line. Ever watch football?"

Char rolled her eyes. "On Sundays. I don't like it."

Steph nodded. "You know those funny dances the players do when they make a touchdown? That was your dad when he won a race."

Char giggled.

Gabe shook his head, frowning down into his coffee, but one corner of his mouth hitched upward. "Yeah, thanks for that."

She nudged him playfully with her elbow. "And funny. I could never stay mad at him 'cause he always made me laugh."

Molly leaned her hands on the counter and smiled. "I'm dying to hear how you two met."

Steph's chest grew heavy. Of course he hadn't ever mentioned her to his family. Because he'd clearly forgotten all about her. He'd moved on. And while some part of her understood, she couldn't deny that the knowledge did, indeed, hurt.

Char paused in the middle of spreading cream cheese on the bagel and looked up, brows raised. "Please?"

Who was she to deny them?

* * *

Two hours later, she stood with Gabe on the front porch. He'd walked her to the door, pulled her outside, and closed the door behind them.

As she stood alone with him now, even after the great breakfast with his daughter, an awkward awareness floated around them. She'd spent the last two days making love to this man. They'd eaten together, showered together. Now? Their weekend was officially over, and her stomach tightened at the thought of not seeing him again.

He reached out as if to touch her, hesitated, then stuffed his hands in his pockets. "I'd kiss you, but the blinds are open behind me. Chances are, they're in there watching us."

Steph leaned sideways enough to peek around him. He was right. Molly and Char stood in the living room, heads bent together, gazes darting back and forth to the window.

Steph laughed. "Yup. I'm betting you get the third degree as soon as I leave. You'll just have to settle for a hug."

When she opened her arms, he stepped into them,

wrapping his tightly around her. He held her there a moment before turning his head to kiss her cheek. His voice came warm and husky in her ear. "Thank you. I owe you for that."

"Nope. You'd have done the same for me." She held on to him for a moment longer than necessary. "It was good seeing you, Gabe."

He pulled back first and released her, once again stuffing his hands in his pockets. Deep grooves formed between his brows, regret taking shape in his gaze. "Take care of yourself, Steph."

"You too." Heart sinking into her heels, she rested a hand against his chest and leaned up on her toes to press a kiss to his stubbled cheek. Then she squared her shoulders and forced herself to turn away. They'd agreed on a weekend, and it was over. Exactly as it should be.

* * *

"Soo..." Mandy plopped unceremoniously down onto the couch beside Steph, her face lit up like a child's on Halloween night. "How was it? Come on. Spill."

Seated on the love seat kitty-corner to the couch, Lauren grinned. Her eyes twinkled with merriment and mischief. "Elise told me you brought a hunk into my shop. Too bad I missed him."

Steph sighed and rolled her eyes, but she couldn't contain a grin of her own. A few hours after she'd gotten home from Gabe's, Mandy and Lauren had arrived on her doorstep. Lauren had been holding a white bakery box, which meant she'd brought goodies. Mandy's face had held a telltale grin, which meant they'd come for "the deets." The moment they'd entered her apartment, they'd berated her for having ignored their mountain of calls and texts over the weekend. Then they began with the twenty questions.

Steph shrugged. "Not much *to* tell. He was nice."

At some point she'd have to tell them the truth, but she didn't want to think about it, let alone talk about it. She knew two things for positive. One, that Gabe had gotten to her. For a few blissful days, she'd gotten to see him, talk to him, indulge her senses. And it had reminded her of all the minute reasons she'd fallen in love with him years ago. In fact, she was pretty sure she liked him better now.

She also knew her best friends. These two would try to talk her into seeing him again, and she couldn't let that happen or she'd end up where she'd already been—in love with a man who couldn't love her back. She'd gotten what she wanted from this weekend, but she was having to leave him behind for the second time. And just like eleven years ago, it was an ache in her chest she didn't know what to do with.

When she wasn't forthcoming, Mandy blinked at her. "That's it? That's all we get? You were gone all weekend and all I get is a 'he was nice?' I'm assuming you spent the weekend with him, because you didn't answer my calls."

Steph grinned, reached for her cup, seated on the coffee table, and attempted to distract her best friend. "All ten thousand of them."

Mandy pursed her lips and leaned forward, snatching a chocolate chip cookie from the box on the table. "Oh, it wasn't ten thousand."

Steph laughed and sipped at her now lukewarm coffee. "No, only a dozen."

Lauren flashed a sugar-sweet smile. "Come on. Spending an entire weekend with someone isn't like you, and I'm dying to know. How was he? Was he what you hoped? Was he different from the rest?"

Steph held up a free hand and laughed. "All right, all right. I'll dish." She bit her bottom lip, then squeezed her eyes closed. She'd have to let them in on the truth sooner or later. Might as well be now. "Gabe."

It was awful to tease, but she had no idea what their reaction would be when she told them who, exactly, her date had been. Her jangling nerves told her she didn't want to know.

"Gabe who?" As expected, Lauren's question filled with recognition and suspicion.

Steph sighed and opened her eyes, forcing herself to face the two of them. "Donovan."

Lauren's mouth dropped open, brows shooting up into her hairline. She leaned forward, depositing her cup onto the coffee table. "Oh my God. Trent's Gabe?"

Steph nodded and leaned back, resting her head against the couch. "He and I knew each other in college. I haven't seen him in eleven years. All this damn time and it turns out he's been living right around the corner."

"I've only met him a handful of times, but Gabe is seriously hot." Mandy nudged her foot. "I'm dying to know...How was he?"

Steph couldn't resist a giggle. Mandy's eyes gleamed with playful impishness and girlish camaraderie. God, she loved these women.

"You can't tell anybody." She darted a glance between them and then pointed at Lauren. "Especially Trent. The last thing I need is for us to end up the topic of gossip."

Lauren made a crisscross motion over her heart but gave a sympathetic frown and shook her head. "Of course, but for what it's worth, Trent would never tell anybody. It's not his style."

Mandy just shrugged. "Who do I have left to tell?"

"Thank you." Steph closed her eyes, memories from the night before moving through her mind like movie clips. Gabe's mouth on her body. His hands on her ass, pulling her to him. A hot little shiver moved over the surface of her skin, and God help her, a sigh worthy of a high school girl with a crush escaped her. "He still melts my knees. Hell. Who am I kidding? He melts my everything."

Mandy giggled.

"Are you going to see him again?" Lauren asked.

There it was. The question she'd known one of the girls would ask sooner or later. She wasn't any more ready for it now, though, than she had been the night of her date.

Steph opened her eyes and jerked upright, taking a sip of her coffee before answering. "No."

Mandy pursed her lips. "Why the hell not? You haven't gotten that look about any man since Alec."

"For one, he has a daughter, and second, he's still mourning his wife's death, which is how it should be, but it means he's got 'complicated' written all over him." She swirled her mug, watching the last of the caramel-colored liquid slosh in the cup. "I'll admit it. I agreed to go with you guys to Military Match because I wanted something more. I'm tired of being alone. I'll even admit Gabe was everything I needed this weekend. But I can't allow myself to get wrapped up in him again."

Both girls went eerily quiet and exchanged suspicious glances. Lauren shot her a worried frown, but being the shy one of their trio, seemed to be holding her tongue. Steph had no desire to go back to one-night stands, and they both knew it.

Mandy laid a hand on her leg. "Honey, the first man you've met in two years who you want to see again and you're not going to because he's exactly what you want?"

Steph couldn't hold back her grin. Damn it all to hell. Leave it to Mandy to make it all sound so simple. "Pretty much."

Mandy shook her head, sending her dark curls bouncing around her chin, and furrowed her brow. "How the hell does that make any sense?"

Steph laughed at the blunt observation and turned a raised brow at Mandy. "This coming from the woman who has a crush on her brother's boss and won't tell him."

Mandy's face turned as red as a fresh, ripe Red Delicious apple. She stuck her nose in the air and reached for another cookie from the box on the table. "Marcus Denali doesn't even know I'm alive."

Mandy had had a crush on Marcus from the first day she'd met him. Steph couldn't blame the poor girl. Like the rest of the guys who worked at the motorcycle shop, he was ex-military and all muscle. Unfortunately, though, despite Mandy's shameless flirting, he hadn't given her the time of day so far.

Lauren took sudden interest in her coffee cup. Ever the

polite one, she took an extended moment to sip carefully at her coffee before speaking again. "Food. Entice their appetites and you'll get their other appetite going, if you catch my drift."

Mandy grinned from ear to ear. "And this coming from the virgin."

"*Ex*-virgin, thank you very much." The corners of Lauren's mouth twitched. "And I'm telling you, it works every time. Trent even admitted that his attraction to me started because I force-fed him chocolate. I brought him dinner and dessert one night, and as usual, he was grumpy. So I told him he clearly needed to eat and shoved one in his mouth. Heck, that month we spent together, we'd often meet for dinner and it would lead...*elsewhere*."

Mandy let out a quiet groan and pinched the bridge of her nose. "Forgive me. I'm ecstatic you and Trent are together and so disgustingly happy, but I do *not* want to know the details of my brother's sex life."

Steph laughed and leaned back, crossing one leg over the other. "She's right, though. Fill a man's belly, and he's yours. Find out his favorites and cook him up some."

Lauren winked at Mandy. "It just so happens Marcus is a sucker for a good homemade chocolate chip cookie. I can teach you to make them, but really, if you can follow a recipe, you can make cookies."

"That's a nice thought and all, sweetie, but I caught a conversation between Marcus and the guys from the shop a couple weeks ago. Trent had them order me a part I needed to fix my bike, and when I went to pick it up, the guys were teasing Marcus about his latest conquest. Some bottle blonde with big boobs from the sound of it." Mandy rolled her eyes and waved a hand over herself. "And here I am, a five-foot-two-inch, curly-haired brunette who can go jogging without a bra."

Lauren shot Mandy a mischievous grin as she bit into a cookie. "I wasn't Trent's type either."

Mandy flushed to the roots of her dark hair but turned to Steph, brows raised. "Is that what you did with Gabe? Enticed him with food?"

Steph gave a half-hearted shrug. "It wasn't planned, but sort of. We had dinner and took dessert back to his place. It's what we used to do, back in college. Dinner and a movie. Just without the movie this time."

Lauren set her cookie on a paper napkin on her leg, her expression sobering as she glanced at Steph. "Why don't you want to see him again? I mean, if you've got history and the chemistry is still there, it seems to me he'd be the perfect person to find your feet with again." She shrugged.

Steph drew a deep breath and released it. "I had to watch him walk away from me once, when his parents died, and I can't do it again. A weekend fling with a nice guy? That I can handle. A step in the right direction, you know? But I'd be nothing more than a rebound to him. Better to end it now while I'm still in control than later when I'm lost in him all over again."

"You know." Coffee cup in hand, Lauren rose from her seat and maneuvered her way around the furniture, heading for the kitchen. "You could always do what I did. Give him a month and see how it goes. You were friends once, right?"

"Yes, but I ended up falling for him." Steph pushed off the

couch, following Lauren. "Besides. I remember how miserable you were when that month ended."

Lauren paused in the middle of refilling her mug to glance over her shoulder. "Because I missed him. But I didn't regret it. Not a single moment. Not even at the end."

Steph opened her mouth to voice a protest, but Lauren shook her head and held up a hand.

"All I'm suggesting is that you enjoy him for a while." She picked up her mug, winking as she passed Steph on her return to the living room.

Steph refilled her cup, but Lauren's suggestion wouldn't leave her mind. Was she right? She and Trent had started out as friends. Military Match pairing them together had almost seemed like an omen. Lauren had gone into that date intending to lose her virginity to a nice guy and had, in the end, asked Trent to be her first lover. It was how their month-long fling had started.

But could Steph do the same thing with Gabe? Could she go back to what they'd had in college, hot sex with no strings attached? That was the problem. She didn't know if she could. Not without falling for him all over again.

Lauren reclaimed her spot on the love seat, tucked one leg beneath her, and looked between Steph and Mandy. "So you guys are coming to the engagement party, right?"

"Wouldn't miss it for the world." Steph shot a smile over her shoulder as she poured a measure of creamer into her cup, then followed Lauren back into the living room.

Mandy raised her brows. "It's Saturday, right?"

Lauren nodded as she sipped at her coffee. "At your parents' place."

"Mom's taking over, I assume?" Mandy rolled her eyes.

Lauren let out a soft laugh. "Like she did with Will and Skylar, yeah. We're letting her. It makes her happy, which makes Trent happy, and it takes the pressure off me. We want to keep it simple, though. Just close friends and family." She peered over at Steph, eyes glittering with mischief. "Which means Trent invited the guys from the shop."

Dread sank, hard and cold, in her stomach. So Gabe would be there.

She'd have to see him again, would have to shove down the overwhelming desire that would no doubt flare again at her first glance of him.

Desperate to distract herself from *that* particular line of thinking, she waggled her brows. "Now, about the bachelorette party..."

CHAPTER EIGHT

Gabe slotted the plate into the dishwasher, tossing a smile at Molly as he reached into the sink for another. "Thanks for offering to take Char tonight. Trent said she was more than welcome to come, but I think she'd have a better time with you and the kids."

"No problem." Molly, standing beside him in the kitchen, scrubbed at another plate, her gaze on her task. "So. Steph's nice. I like her. Char did, too. Have you seen her this week?"

Gabe swallowed a miserable groan. She had to ask that. After their parents died, he and Molly had come to rely on each other. There really wasn't anything they'couldn't talk about. The first time she'd contemplated having sex, they'd had an open and frank discussion about it. When he had a big decision to make, he usually ran it by her first.

But this wasn't something he wanted to discuss. He was trying not to think about Steph. Or look forward to seeing her tonight. Tonight was Trent and Lauren's engagement party. He knew damn well Steph would be there, and damned if that didn't have every drop of blood in his body on a low boil. Even though he knew he shouldn't be, he couldn't remember the last time he'd been this excited about anything.

"I've been pretty busy." Hoping she'd give up, he gave a noncommittal shrug and reached for another plate from the sink in front of him, slotting it into the dishwasher.

Never one to be deterred, however, Molly set the now rinsed plate into the left half of the divided sink and nudged him with an elbow. "Don't think I didn't notice the way you avoided me after she left on Sunday. Inquiring minds want to know. *Do* you plan to see her again?"

Gabe sighed. So much for getting her to leave it alone. "She's just an old friend."

"Right. And I'm Abe Lincoln." Molly set the last dish into the second sink, then shut off the water and picked up a small towel, turning to him as she dried her hands. "You want to see her again. Admit it."

He set the last plate into the dishwasher, then reached beneath the sink for the soap and filled the dispenser, using the chore as excuse not to face Molly's fishing expedition. "It was a temporary thing."

Molly quirked a brow. "And now?"

Just that fast, the memories flooded over him. Standing with Steph, here in the kitchen. The glint in her eyes when she'd smeared that frosting across his lips. The addicting rush of her kiss.

Along with it came a confusion he didn't know what to do with. Every time he passed Julia's picture on the dresser, guilt formed a hard knot in his gut. No matter how he tried to convince himself he'd needed that weekend, it still felt like he'd cheated on his wife.

Exactly why he was trying not to think about Steph. And here was Molly, bringing it all back up.

He leaned against the counter and folded his arms. "Fine. You really want to know? I'd forgotten what it's like not to have to sleep alone. That's the part I hate the most, having to crawl into bed alone at night. And the sex?" He reached up and rubbed the back of his neck. "Hell. Sex with an actual woman is never a bad thing."

For a couple of days, he'd forgotten the pain and monotony his life had become. Steph had made him forget, and she'd made him feel alive again. But that she'd actually stayed Sunday morning to help ease a difficult situation had been the nail in his proverbial coffin. She didn't have to do that. Not everybody would have. Despite her emphatic protest about boundaries, she'd stayed, because deep down she had a good heart. That made her...irresistible.

Molly laughed and shook her head. "Honestly, Gabe. Need to know."

Gabe chuckled and bumped her shoulder. "Don't ask questions you don't want the answers to, then, Miss Nosy."

Molly sobered, softness and gentle understanding moving over her features. "So why don't you want to see her again?"

He blew out a defeated breath and shook his head. "I've been asking myself that damn question all week. I have an entire list of reasons why, the top of which is that Steph wants something long-term and I can't give it to her. Not yet. And I think she deserves more. I hurt her enough in the past. But I won't deny that I'd kill to see her again."

Molly studied him for a long moment, as if weighing a decision. As if searching for something within him. Whatever it was, seconds later she seemed to arrive at her conclusion because she straightened off the counter and faced him. She laid a hand against his shoulder. "Far be it from me to stick my nose in where it doesn't belong..."

He laughed. "Hasn't ever stopped you before."

She narrowed her eyes, but the corners of her mouth twitched. "It doesn't have to be complicated. She clearly likes *you*, and—"

"I should hope so."

Molly rolled her eyes. "Would you let me finish a sentence, please?"

He rolled his eyes right back at her and waved a hand in her direction. "Fine. Go ahead. Lecture me."

Molly punched him lightly in the shoulder. "Spend time with her. Enjoy her. Even Char seems to like her."

Exactly what he'd hoped she wouldn't suggest. The hard part was, he hadn't a damn clue what the answer was.

"I can't promise her forever, or anything like it, and I won't use her that way. She was a friend once, and she hasn't had it easy either. She deserves better." He refused to treat her the way the rest of the men in her life had, but if he gave in to the lure of her, that's all he would be. Just another asshole on her list. Hell. He already was.

Molly pinned him with a direct, probing stare. "Did she *ask* you for forever?"

"No. It was for the weekend only, and it was her idea."

"Then stop overthinking this and run with it." Molly rubbed a hand over his shoulder. "Julia's death was hard, I know. It came at an awful time. You were still struggling with the loss of your leg, and it was a shock to you and Char both, but Julia would want you to move on, and you know it. So I'm going to tell you the same thing I told you after you lost your leg. I love you, Gabe, but it's time to get up and learn to walk again."

She kissed his cheek, then moved out of the kitchen, disappearing down the hallway toward Char's room.

He was getting a lecture on his love life from his baby sister. It used to be the other way around. The worst part was, she was right. Goddamn it.

* * *

Gabe turned his head, scanning the yard around him. Trent and Lauren's engagement party turned out to be small and intimate, less than fifty people or so, mostly family and close friends, but Trent's parents had gone all out. A live local band played what sounded like jazz. Across the lawn a buffet table and a makeshift bar had been set up. He and the guys were seated around a small table in the backyard. Trent, Marcus, and Mike were discussing their latest project at the shop.

Gabe couldn't concentrate worth a damn. Steph had been in his peripheral all evening. No matter how much he tried to stay focused on the guys' conversation, his gaze invariably ended up back on her. She, Lauren, and Mandy, along with half a dozen others, were currently out in the designated dance space, set up beyond the band, chatting and watching them play.

He couldn't stop soaking her in. She looked phenomenal. Her long dress skimmed her curves and fell to her ankles, sexy without revealing anything. She didn't appear to have panty lines, and the thought that she might not be wearing any panties made his cock ache.

The music changed, moving from upbeat to soft, slow strains that brought to mind making love.

"That's my cue, gentlemen. Maybe a whirl around the dance floor with my girl will help get rid of this damn headache." Trent pushed out of his seat, giving them a two-fingered salute before making his way toward the crowd.

Out on the dance floor, couples paired off. Steph turned and made her way to the buffet table. There, she picked up a flute of champagne and stood watching the couples with an almost wistful expression.

Marcus nudged Gabe's elbow, jerking him from his perusal. "Man, if you don't go ask her to dance, I'm going to. A woman that beautiful should not have to watch from the sidelines."

Marcus had a point, of course. Not once in the last two hours had he stopped thinking about Molly's suggestion. Being in the same space with Steph provided a temptation he only *just* managed to resist. But he still had no desire to use her as his stepping-stone. Dating was one thing. Steph was entirely another.

He shook his head. He'd just make an ass of himself. "I couldn't find a groove if you handed me one."

Marcus pushed to his feet, making clucking noises under his breath as he walked toward the buffet table. Steph faced him as he came to a stop beside her. He extended his left hand, which she accepted with a gentle smile and a nod, and he led her toward the couples already gathered.

It wasn't until Marcus pulled her close that the green-eyed monster finally made its appearance. He knew damn well Marcus was goading him. As he swayed her around in a circle, Marcus pulled her a little too close, tossing Gabe an arrogant wink over her shoulder as he settled his grubby paws on her lower back. Just above her ass.

Gabe rolled his eyes but pushed to his feet and made his way in their direction. Steph could do worse than Marcus, but the sight of her in someone else's arms rubbed his nerves raw. Besides. It was just dancing. He could dance with a friend. Right?

As he came up behind Steph, Marcus grinned. Ear to fucking ear.

Gabe tried for a glare, but damned if he could keep the corners of his mouth from twitching as he jerked a thumb over his shoulder. "You're a cocky son of a bitch, Denali. Beat it, would you?"

Steph turned sideways to look at him. Heat flared in her eyes, fueling the fire burning in his belly. Just that fast his cock thickened, pressing almost painfully against his zipper. Great. Now he had a hard-on, and he couldn't even adjust the damn thing or he'd draw attention to it.

Grinning in triumph now, Marcus had the audacity to wink as he moved around Steph, heading for the tables again. "Knew that'd get your cowardly ass over here."

Gabe shot Marcus another glare before turning to Steph. He offered a smile and held out his hand. "Care to dance?"

Steph nodded. "I'd love to."

He gripped her waist, tugging her close, and she settled her palms against his pecs. For several beats, only the soft strains of the music filled the space between them. Not once did she look away, and all too soon he lost every thought in his head in her. Her breasts pushed into his chest. Her thighs brushed his as they moved, her lean stomach brushing the front placket of his jeans. His cock hardened to painful proportions, though if she noticed, she didn't say anything.

After a few beats, she smiled. "Why didn't you just come ask me yourself?"

His gut tightened. "Because I wasn't planning to ask. I—"

She stiffened in his arms. Hurt flared in her eyes, and she braced her hands against his chest and shoved. "Don't do me any favors, Gabe."

His heart hammered like a runaway freight train. Great, he'd offended her. *Way to go, dumbass.*

He tightened his grip on her and pulled her back, though she didn't relax in his embrace. "Let me finish. We agreed on a weekend. We're only here together by accident. Because we have the same friends. Besides. I didn't want to intrude. But then I saw you with Marcus, and I couldn't help myself."

When the tension finally eased in her body, Gabe allowed himself to breathe again.

Steph shook her head. "How the hell did I miss that you were so damn close all this time?"

One corner of his mouth twitched. He'd asked himself that same question at least a thousand times over the last week. "Damned if I know. Must've been fate."

She gave a playful roll of her eyes. "Tell me you don't believe in fate."

He lifted a brow. "We're here, aren't we?"

Steph's gaze danced over his face, though she remained silent, and several tension-filled seconds passed. Clearly she searched for something, but what? Scratch that. He didn't want to know.

Seeming to find what she looked for, she shifted closer, slid her hands around his rib cage and up his back, and rested her cheek against his chest. Unable to resist the pull of her, he wrapped his arms around her in return, rested his cheek against the top of her head, and let himself have the moment. Just being in her presence soothed the lonely ache deep inside. Maybe if he was lucky, tonight he'd actually sleep.

It wasn't long before everything else around him faded as he slowly lost himself in her. Her soft, feminine scent curled around his senses, the warmth of her body pulling him in until there wasn't anything left *but* her.

"Gabe?"

Her voice drifted into the miniscule space between them barely above a whisper, half murmured into his chest. There was a sleepy edge to it that suggested she was as lost as he was. God help them both.

"Yeah?"

"I wouldn't have minded if you'd intruded."

He stifled a groan and turned his head, pressing a kiss to her temple. She'd had to go and say that. "You're killing me, babe. You look good in that dress, you know."

"Just good?"

The subtle tease in her voice pulled a chuckle out of him.

"I'm pretty sure you know exactly how good I think you look." He turned his mouth to her ear and lowered his voice so only she would hear him. He shouldn't keep this line of questioning going, but neither could he resist her. "I've been hard since I got here."

Steph lifted her head, stared for a beat, then leaned her head beside his ear. Her lips moved against the lobe, her warm breath whispering over the skin of his neck. "Then I suppose it wouldn't be good to mention that you in those jeans is enough to make me wet."

He swallowed a groan. Damned if he could resist that either, which she no doubt knew. "Your panties, you mean?"

Mischief glinted in her eyes as she pulled back. "Who says I'm wearing any?"

His cock twitched. The little minx. "Keep it up, sweetheart."

She looked down, swirled her finger over his chest. "Or?"

Or he'd do something he'd regret. Like pull her into the house, find a secluded room, and hike that dress above her waist.

He clenched his jaw. Every muscle in his body tensed, and his jeans were attempting to strangle him. If he didn't change the subject and soon, he was going to do all of that and then some. "You're in fine form tonight, Steph. Are you drunk?"

Steph let out a breathless laugh. "No. Just having fun. My best friend is getting married. How can you not get caught up in the excitement? Look at them."

She nodded off to her left, and he followed her gaze. Lauren and Trent were wrapped around each other like vines, swaying like the lovers they were to the gentle strains of the song. Gabe's chest tightened. God, he missed that.

Determined not to let the grief suck him under, he turned

back to Steph, forcing his mind to focus on the conversation. "Because you want something permanent."

She shrugged, her gaze still on Lauren and Trent. "I gave up trying to find it for a while, but seeing them made me want it again. What they have is rare. Not everybody gets a happily ever after, and I'm still not sure I'll find it, but I want it all same."

Gabe clenched his jaw as irritation prickled along his skin. He knew from the things she'd told him that someone had hurt her, and he had the sudden desire to break the guy's jaw. That she'd given up on love entirely made his chest ache as well. She deserved what Lauren and Trent had found. "Maybe you were just dating the wrong kinds of men."

"Maybe."

He wanted to ask what she meant by that, but the music changed. The couples around them dispersed, bodies picking up the new, livelier beat. They both stopped moving, but neither one let go. He wasn't sure he could.

Steph studied him, eyes searching and vulnerable. After a moment she gave him a tender smile and stepped back. "Thanks for the dance."

She didn't give him a chance to respond, but turned and walked off toward the house, her gait slow but steady. For a moment he could only watch her go. He wanted a million different things right then. To drag her into a dark corner and bury himself in her velvet heat. To get lost in the heady press of her warm skin and those phenomenal sounds she made in the throes of an orgasm.

But mostly? He wanted the bliss. Just being near her had made the crowd disappear for a while. Along with the last three years and the empty ache he'd carried around for so long he feared it would be there forever.

There was just her. Wherever the hell their relationship led him, he wanted to follow it. The question was, could he let himself?

As she disappeared into the house, his answer came every bit as easily as the question. He could. He had to take this step at some point, release the guilt over Char and Julia and date someone for real, have something more than a weekend fling. Who better to do it with than Steph? Someone who knew *him*, in all his brokenness and idiosyncrasies.

Could he do it without hurting her, though? He didn't know. All he did know was that for the first time since Julia's death, he didn't feel so...broken. What harm could come from extending their time together? Enjoying each other in the here and now and simply...seeing where it went?

Now he just had to convince her that they could be good for each other.

CHAPTER NINE

Steph opened a cabinet in search of a glass. A row of clear tumblers sat neatly on the shelf, and she pulled one down, filling it from the tap. She wasn't really thirsty, but she needed a moment to collect herself. Her mind was running on overtime. Like eleven years ago, her heart wanted to get hung up on Gabe. He was a good guy, but he'd still broken her heart. Simply being in the same space with him had all those emotions she didn't want to deal with rising to the surface all over again. The unbelievable need. The yearning to be closer to him in all possible ways.

If she wanted a real relationship, she'd have to learn to let someone in again. She just didn't know if she could do it with him. No matter how much she regretted not telling him how she felt.

The sliding glass doors opened behind her, and the noise from the backyard rushed in, then closed out again. Steph took a sip of the water, letting it cool her parched throat, and turned her head to see who'd followed her inside.

Her heart skipped a beat. Gabe made his way in her direction, his brow set in determination. Hands beginning to shake, she turned to the small window over the sink and sipped at her water. Her ears homed in on the sound of his footsteps as he crossed the kitchen.

When his scent curled around her, she instinctively knew he stood right behind her, but she couldn't move. She barely remembered the in and out of breathing. How could a simple weekend bring her back to this place, where she needed him so damn much?

He stroked a finger along her shoulder, his touch so light he set off a shower of goose bumps that shivered all the way down her spine. "I want to see you again."

Steph closed her eyes. Swallowed past the lump stuck in her throat. God, he'd had to tell her that. Did she *want* to see him again? In a heartbeat. If only to feel half of what she did when she was with him. Free. Accepted. Adored. But she'd be little more than a rebound to him. Eventually this would end. He'd walked away from her once already. Would she have the strength to watch him do it again?

She shook her head. "I'm sorry, but I don't think it's a good idea."

He reached around her, took the glass from her fingers and set it on the counter. Then he took her hand, tugging her behind him as he made his way through the kitchen and around the corner. Once out of sight of the sliding glass doors, he turned to her and pressed her back against a wall. He didn't give her time to form a coherent response or even to think of one, but settled his mouth on hers.

His lips tangled with hers, his tongue flicking along her

bottom lip, asking the ancient question. Helpless to do anything else, she opened for him, and he plunged in on a quiet groan that rumbled through his chest. Her hands slid around his rib cage and up his back, her body soaking in his unbelievable warmth, and he leaned into her, rocking his hips into hers.

In seconds he had her a shivering, hot pool of need, the ache between her thighs so keen she wanted to weep. Such was her need for him. It always had been. He knew exactly what she liked, what she needed, and God help her, her body responded.

The only man in eleven years with the capacity to make her forget herself, Alec included. Alec had been safe.

Gabe didn't give her time to approve or deny his assault—not that she could—but nibbled his way across her lips to her jaw. "I've been trying to resist you, Steph, but I can't. Tell me you don't want me the way I want you and I'll leave this here. But I think you want the same thing I do, and I don't see any reason why we can't indulge for a while."

She *ought* to remove the temptation right here and push him away, go back outside and find Lauren and Mandy. But his mouth skimmed her neck and along the exposed skin of her shoulder with the lightness of butterfly wings. She couldn't think much past the desperate need to hear him describe his desires. "And what is it you want?"

His hands claimed a hold on her ass, pulling her tight against him. "This."

A quiet gasp escaped her. No way could she mistake his meaning. His erection had to be straining the zipper on his jeans, because it settled, thick and hard, against her stomach. A little shift of fabric and he could be inside her, easing the ache he'd created.

"I want to bury myself inside of you. I want these sweet thighs wrapped around my hips, and God, Steph, I want to hear you moan my name. As often I can." His big, warm hands caressed the front of her thighs as his tongue slid up the side of her neck. "But you know what I really want, sweetheart?"

His warm palm cupped her mound and his deft fingers found her clit through her dress, pressing with the exact right amount of pressure. Pleasure erupted through her, and her whole body lit up. A quiet moan left her, and her knees wobbled.

"I want to taste you. I want to bury my mouth in your cunt and feel you come all over my tongue. Oh, I remember the way you taste. So sweet and musky." He let out an agonized groan. "The way your hands would fist in my hair and pull me in. You'd ride my mouth. God, that's bliss."

On some plane of existence, she knew he was taunting her. She couldn't remember the last time she'd heard him use the word "cunt." Gabe might be a SEAL and a little rough around the edges, but he was polite. Always.

Never mind that Trent's whole family—along with fifty other people—sat just outside. Anyone could come in here and find them. Still, the husky rumble of Gabe's voice against her skin proved a stronger lure. Sensation conspired against her, and her thighs spread of their own accord. Her hand joined his, pressing his fingers deeper into her. A wave of luscious heat slid through her, loosening her joints. Perspiration prickled along her skin. Her hips rocked in time with his motions, sending pleasure flooding her veins. In no time at all, he had her body riding that fine, sweet edge.

She bit her lower lip hard to keep the moans pent up in her throat from leaving her mouth.

Just as suddenly as he started, Gabe removed his hand and stepped back, leaving her teetering on the edge of an orgasm. Breathless and shaking, she opened her heavy-lidded eyes and met his gaze.

"We want the same things, baby. Someone to find our feet with. I want more time with you. I'm not quite done with you yet." He brushed his thumb along her lower lip, then followed the path with his mouth. "You want someone you can trust, and despite everything, I hope you know you *can* trust me."

Steph swallowed to wet her parched throat, but she couldn't force her tongue to work and nodded instead. That part she couldn't deny. She did trust him. Just not with her heart.

"I don't see why we can't enjoy each other for a while. When it no longer suits either of our needs, it ends. Think about it." He brushed another barely there kiss across her mouth, then released her and disappeared around the corner, his quiet footsteps fading away from her.

Steph sagged back against the wall and closed her eyes, gulping in breaths in an attempt to cool down. No way in hell could she could go back outside looking the way she did. No doubt she looked wanton and half fucked, because she sure as hell felt that way. She doubted her knees would hold her up anyway.

God, he'd had to go and lay that on the table. How the

hell did she turn him down when she couldn't deny she wanted him?

* * *

Steph curled her fingers around the deck's wooden railing and nudged Lauren, standing on her right, with an elbow. "Nice view down there."

The party had begun to wind down. Most of the guests had already left, save for a few stragglers. She, Mandy, and Lauren were watching the action down in the yard, as Gabe, Trent, Mike, and Marcus packed up the tables and chairs. Watching Gabe's biceps flex wasn't doing her determination to keep her distance from him any good.

Lauren blushed.

"Yes. Yes, it is." Mandy, on her left, let out an Oscar-worthy sigh, then glanced at Steph. "Saw you dancing with Gabe earlier. You two looked pretty cozy."

Steph's face burned. There was no getting anything past these two. She waved a hand in dismissal. "It was just a dance."

Mandy snorted. "Yeah, and I'm not standing here watching Marcus's fine ass flex in those *delicious* jeans."

Lauren giggled. "And Trent was just a fling."

Steph sighed and relented. "I'll admit he made me an...*indecent proposal*, if you will." Desperate to steer this conversation anywhere else, Steph laid a hand on Mandy's arm. "You don't have to fall in love with the guy to enjoy all those muscles, you know."

Mandy let out a heavy sigh. "I'm not even on his radar."

Steph nodded at the yard. "So *make* him notice."

Mandy stared for a moment, as if lost in thought, then glanced at Steph. "I'll tell you what. I'll take my chances if you will."

Lauren looked over at her, her expression somber. "I didn't regret my time with Trent."

Steph pushed away from the railing and shook her head. "That's my cue to go."

Mandy cocked a brow. "What's the matter—you aren't *chicken*, are you?"

The taunt in Mandy's tone had Steph biting back a smile. No way in hell could she resist, and Mandy knew it.

She folded her arms and arched a brow. "You first."

Truth was, she had no intention of taking Gabe up on his offer. She was just trying to give Mandy a little push in the right direction. Help her to find her courage. With two older brothers and a mother who insisted girls could do anything boys could, Mandy normally wasn't afraid of anything. Marcus, however, made her tuck tail and run.

Mandy's mouth dropped open. She darted a glance at the yard. "In front of everybody?"

"You aren't *chicken*, are you?" Steph quirked a brow. When Mandy just stared, Steph let out a quiet laugh and jabbed a finger in her direction. "You started that."

Mandy drew her shoulders back and marched past them. Chin jutting at a determined angle, she stormed down the deck stairs and across the yard to where the men were cleaning up the last set of table and chairs. She stopped behind Marcus and tapped him on the shoulder. Gabe, Mike, and Trent halted in their task, looking up as Marcus turned in her direction.

"Holy crap." Steph covered her mouth, giggling behind her fingers. "She's actually doing it."

Too curious to see exactly how far her headstrong best friend would take their taunt, Steph couldn't stop watching. Sure enough, Mandy peered up at Marcus, who stood a good head and shoulders above her, then gripped his face in her palms, lifted onto her toes, and sealed her mouth over his. The kiss was little more than a lingering peck, and she did an immediate about-face, but she'd done it.

As Mandy hightailed it toward the deck, the guys all turned to watch her go. A full-on grin spread across Trent's face. Gabe tipped his head back and laughed. Marcus rolled his eyes, but one corner of his mouth quirked upward.

Mandy trotted up the deck stairs, eyes wide and round, face as white as an Easter lily.

"Oh my freaking God. I cannot believe I just did that." Mandy let out an insane little giggle as she strode past, heading for the sliding glass doors leading into the house. "Your turn."

She yanked the sliding glass door open and disappeared inside the house moments later. Steph and Lauren broke into a fit of giggles. Lauren snorted, then giggled some more before finally turning and following Mandy into the house. Steph watched her go for a moment. That challenge had been of the high school variety for sure, but damned if she could be sorry for it. Not for the first time tonight, she felt free and unfettered, too caught up in the camaraderie to think about Gabe's proposal.

Of course, Mandy's little challenge meant she had to go through with her end of the bargain. She had to agree to

Gabe's proposal. The thought had the butterflies starting in her stomach. A fling with Gabe wouldn't exactly be a hardship, and she damn well knew it. But could she do it and not lose her heart in the process?

* * *

Ten minutes later, after saying a quick good-bye to the girls, Steph made her way out to her car, parked on the street in front of the house. She climbed inside, setting her purse on the passenger seat, put the key in the ignition, and turned it. A soft *click* sounded through the interior, but the car didn't roar to life the way it was supposed to.

She cursed under her breath. Her piece-of-shit Ford. She'd had her Mustang for five years now. It had run great when she'd test-driven it, but she'd had nothing but trouble with it since.

"Come on, you piece of crap. Just get me home." She turned the key again. The same *click* sounded, and again the engine failed to start. The dashboard lights dimmed, the battery warning light blazing bright red.

Damn it.

She heaved a sigh and dropped her head back against the seat. Clearly she'd have to hitch a ride from Mandy or Lauren.

Someone tapped on her window. Steph started, jerking her gaze toward the sound. Gabe stood beside the car, brows furrowed. She cracked the door.

Gabe rested his forearm on the roof, leaning down to catch her gaze. "Having trouble?"

"My piece of crap won't start." She waved a hand at the

steering wheel, her face burning. Of all the damn things to happen.

He smiled, polite and amused. "I noticed. Try it again. I want to listen."

She turned the key. The click sounded and again the engine didn't even attempt to turn over.

Gabe pushed away from the car. "Sounds like the starter's okay. Been acting funny?"

She nodded and peered up at him. "The headlights and dash lights are dim, and the power windows won't come down. The check engine light came on a couple days ago, and I had to get a neighbor to jump me tonight before I came over."

He made a sound at the back of his throat. "Pop the hood."

As she bent to pull the lever, Gabe rounded the front fender and strode up the driveway, disappearing into the house. He returned thirty seconds later with Marcus. The security lights on the garage popped on and the door came up. Trent moved out of the space, a flashlight in hand.

Barely a minute later, Mandy and Lauren joined the fray. Steph climbed from the car, her face ablaze as she joined them at the edge of the driveway. She'd always prided herself on making her own way in the world. Now she had six people—six!—surrounding her car. All because the damn thing wouldn't start. It had her fidgeting in her sandals.

As she came to stand beside the girls, Lauren nudged her, nodding in the direction of the men. "Speaking of nice views..."

All three men leaned over Steph's engine, clearly in a world of their own as they discussed her problem. Now, three hot guys bending over an engine ought to be the thrill of a lifetime. Each man kept himself in excellent shape. Bulging biceps and tight jeans-clad rear ends abounded.

"It's enough to make a girl drool." Steph shook her head. "If I weren't so damned embarrassed."

Lauren looped an arm around her shoulders. "Don't be embarrassed, sweetie. It happens to the best of us."

"In fact"—Mandy leaned toward her, hooking an arm around Steph from her other side—"I'm actually rather grateful your car took a crap in front of my parents' house."

"Most definitely." Lauren shot her a sideways grin. "You're getting a special batch of cookies for this."

Down in the street, Trent shined the flashlight into the engine compartment and reached in, fiddled with something, then leaned his elbows on the edge and looked over at the other two men. "Belt looks okay."

Gabe nodded his agreement. "I'll check the solenoid and relay just to be sure, but I'm guessing it's the alternator."

Marcus nodded. "Agreed. I'll call PJ in the morning, see if he can hook us up with the part. For now I'll call Glen and have him tow it to the shop. We can have this fixed for her in an hour."

Steph had finally heard enough. She was a lot of things, but helpless wasn't one of them.

"Um, thanks for the offer, guys, but I can take care of this one on my own." She glanced at Trent. "If it's okay with your parents, the car will have to stay here overnight. I'll call a tow truck in the morning."

Marcus straightened out of the engine compartment and smiled. "It's no problem. We've got the tools at the shop. Save you a bunch on labor *and* the tow truck. Glen owes us a favor anyway."

Gabe shook his head and straightened. "No need. Have Glen tow it to my place. I've got the tools, and I can swing by O'Reilly's for the part. I can take care of it this weekend. Char would love to help me work on this."

Steph shook her head and stepped toward the car. "Really, guys. I don't want to be any more trouble than I already am."

Marcus, however, already had his phone out. "Hey, Glen. I need to call in that favor . . ."

Gabe made his way in her direction. He came to a stop in front of her and hooked his thumbs in his pockets. "It's no trouble, Steph. I've done it for Molly's Escort. I want to make sure Glen has the car. Then I'll take you home."

Steph closed her eyes and pinched the bridge of her nose. She'd officially lost control of her life. Gabe taking her home would force her to accept his proposal. After all, Mandy had held up her end of the bargain.

She dropped her hand and opened her eyes, the weight of the world suddenly pressing down on her. "You don't have to do this."

He smiled. Not just a polite curve of lips, either, but soft and warm and rendering her defenseless in the time it took her to draw a breath. "Nope, I don't, but that's what friends do, right?"

For a moment she could only stare at him. No way was she getting out of this with her heart intact. She could put up all the boundaries in the world. Gabe would just push past all of them. He always had. Deep down he really was a nice guy. Six foot six inches of sexy teddy bear.

Wasn't that what she'd wanted when she'd signed up with that damn dating service in the first place?

Marcus punched a button on his phone, stepping toward Gabe. "Glen says he can be here in twenty."

* * *

Back at her apartment an hour and a half later, Gabe insisted on walking her to her door. God forbid he be like every other man she'd dated and drop her off in the parking lot, so she could get inside without plastering her body to his.

While she pulled out her keys and unlocked her door, he stood quiet and polite behind her, hands tucked in his pockets. After pushing her door open, she finally forced herself to face him. He stared down at her, his expression impassive and hard to read.

So she smiled, because it was all she had the strength to do. "Thank you."

He pulled a hand from his pocket and thumbed her chin. "I'll bring your car back when I have it done tomorrow."

"I could just have Lauren bring me over to get it." At least if Lauren brought her to him, she'd have an excuse not to stay.

Gabe nodded. "Might be best, come to think of it. Just remembered that it's my turn with the girls this weekend."

She arched a brow. She was stalling, which meant she ought to keep her mouth shut and go inside, but damned if she could resist asking. "The girls?"

He nodded. "Every other weekend I take Molly's three girls to give her a break and give her and Leo a chance to be alone for a while. So if I come to you, I'll be lugging four very hyper little girls with me."

"Ah." The sudden desire to see him with the kids, to

watch him in action, swelled behind her breastbone. The feeling was so foreign she almost didn't recognize it. She'd shoved that feeling down that day two years ago when Alec called off the wedding, but she acknowledged it for what it was.

Her soft emotions. The desire for more than the lonely life she'd set for herself. She enjoyed her job, but she saw too much of what went wrong when marriages didn't work out. Had sat in mediations where a couple who'd started out adoring each other could barely stand to be in the same room. Hell, her parents' own marriage had traveled that very road. Then her mother had gotten cancer. Her father drank to numb the guilt he couldn't deal with. Not a single man in her life, Gabe included, had ever wanted to stick around.

All of which meant that whatever the hell she felt now needed to be squashed like a bug.

"Thanks for the ride. I'll see you tomorrow." She flashed what she hoped looked like a polite smile and turned toward her apartment.

"Damn it all to hell."

Gabe's soft curse came seconds before his hand closed around her wrist. He tugged her back as he moved around in front of her. She managed to register the intensity in his eyes before his mouth came down on hers. Gabe wasn't soft and seductive this time. His lips all but bruised hers in his urgency. Her senses filled with him. The warmth and solidness of his body. The slight tremor in his hands as they slid into her hair and fisted there. His mouth slanted over hers, his hot tongue pushing inside, no longer teasing but demanding.

On a shuddering breath, she opened for him, helpless to do anything but.

He let out a quiet groan and leaned into her, rocking his hips against hers. His erection pushed into her stomach, and whatever shred of sanity she'd started with evaporated. Steph slid her hands up his chest, wound her arms around his neck, and lifted onto her toes to get more of him.

When she was melting into him, he finally came up for air. He leaned his forehead against hers and closed his eyes. His jagged breaths matched the fierce thumping of her heart.

"I'm sorry. I should be letting you go, letting you decide all on your own, but damn it. I can't help it. Every time I see you, my cock aches." His mouth moved, skimming across her jawline and down her neck. "Tell me you thought about what I said."

Like she had no willpower at all, she tipped her head to the side, offering herself up to him. Her fingers closed around his T-shirt. "Gabe..."

He lifted his head from her throat, his gaze piercing and intense and obliterating all her defenses. "You're the first, Steph. The first person I've wanted to see in three fucking years. Being with you makes me feel...alive. I know I'm not anything you need or want, but I'm not ready to let you go yet."

She drew her brows together and shook her head, but his mouth closed over hers before she could form any semblance of a response. He brushed his lips across hers, nibbled at the right corner, his touch so damn tender a quiet little whimper escaped her. A freakin' whimper. God, she was toast.

She melted into him again, but this time he released her.

"No rules. When it stops benefiting the both of us, it ends. I would never hurt you, Steph. Just say yes."

How the hell did she say no to that?

CHAPTER TEN

He was shaking. Fucking shaking. His cock throbbed behind his zipper, his need so keen every cell in his body buzzed in anticipation, waiting for Steph to say that magical word.

All because he'd given himself permission to want her, leaving his guts tied in knots and guilt rising like a typhoon over his head. He and Julia had had mutual respect. He'd loved her deeply, but they hadn't *needed* each other. Not like this, where all rational thought gave way to a desire so keen he feared losing all control of himself. Steph was an addiction, and like a junkie, he craved his next high.

He stroked a hand down her cheek, reveling in the incredible softness of her skin. "Tell me you want me the way I want you."

Her eyes danced over his face. In indecision. In torment. Then she sagged back against the wall. "I've always wanted you, Gabe."

That was all he needed to hear. She might be a little gun-shy, but she wanted the same things he did.

He took her hand, pulled her beyond the threshold, taking a moment to close and lock the door, then led her through the living room toward the hallway at the back of her apartment. Once there, he moved inside, stopping at the end of her bed, and turned to her. Gaze locked on hers, he gripped fistfuls of her dress, slowly inching it up her body. He wanted to give her time to protest. Not that she did. Her breathing ramped up a notch, and she lifted her arms, allowing him to pull the dress off over her head. He dropped it at her feet, then hooked her around the waist and tugged her close.

"I believe I owe you an orgasm." He brushed his mouth over hers, then pulled her onto the bed.

She lay down on her back, heavy-lidded eyes full of heat, just watching him. Lying beside her, he trailed his index finger along her collarbone, down between her breasts, and over her stomach. She looked so beautiful lying there, her golden hair a stark contrast to the deep red of her comforter.

He brushed a kiss across her mouth, then worked his way down her body, following the path his fingers had taken.

"You should know I can't stay. Molly always brings the kids over bright and early on her days off. I'll stay as long as I can, but as late as it is, it'll be only a few hours at most." He flicked his gaze to hers as he drew his tongue down the column of her throat, ending in the space between her breasts. "But I knew if I didn't finish what I started earlier there'd be hell to pay later."

He didn't give her time to answer, but moved to her left nipple and sucked it into his mouth. She gasped, her nails gliding along his scalp as her fingers dove into his hair. Taking that as a positive sign, he moved to the other breast to repeat the torture, swirling his tongue around the taut tip, drawing it into his mouth, and sucking hard, the way she liked.

Then he let it pop from his mouth, nipped at the side of her breast, and moved slowly down her belly, heading for her sweet thighs. Every deliberate tease drew a reaction from her. Swirling his tongue down to her belly button made her shiver. Nipping at the soft flesh of her flat stomach made her moan and arch her hips upward.

By the time he'd settled on his belly between her thighs, he was trembling right along with her, his erection pressing painfully against his zipper.

Her thighs parted and bent, opening in silent invitation. "Gabe, please. Don't tease."

He ignored her pleas and stroked the sensitive skin of her inner thighs with his thumbs, letting them graze her lips. She shivered. Moaned. Using his thumbs, he opened her. In the soft light drifting in from the hallway, her sensitive folds glistened with her arousal, her scent filling his nostrils.

He leaned in and, unable to help himself, dipped his tongue inside. Her sweet, musky flavor filled his mouth, and he groaned.

"Christ, I'd forgotten how good you taste." She was sweeter than the ripest summer fruit and all woman. He desperately wanted her thighs to clamp around his ears and his name to leave her lips when she came.

He wanted this to be good for her, though, to remind her how good it was between them, so he needed to go slow.

Luckily, he'd been here before. He knew exactly what it took to make her come so hard she'd lose her breath. So he leaned in again, this time pushing his tongue deep, then dragging it slowly up her slit, and ending with a flick over her engorged clit.

As expected, she groaned from down deep and her hips bucked against his mouth. "Gabe, please..."

He let out a quiet laugh. He hadn't anticipated how aroused she was. He filed the thought away for future reference and flicked her clit again, lightly this time. "Desperate, baby?"

Her fingers fisted in his hair, and her back arched. "Yes!"

He inserted a finger, stroking her inner walls, and peered up at her. "Tell me what you want, Steph."

He could easily give her what she craved. After all, he knew her body as well as his own. But he wanted to hear her say the words.

She was panting, her harsh breaths loud in the otherwise quiet room. Her hips bucked against his ministrations, forcing his finger to slide in and out of her.

"Make me come, Gabe. With your tongue. Your fingers." She let out a needy moan. Her hands dropped to the bed beside her, fingers curling into the comforter beneath her. "You know what to do. *Please.*"

He groaned with her this time. The most erotic sound in the world was her in the throes of an orgasm, and he wanted it almost as badly as she did. Unable to resist any longer, he slid his hands beneath her ass, lifting and angling her, and buried his mouth in her heat.

He'd far underestimated her need. A few flicks of his tongue, and she went rigid beneath him and drew a sharp breath. When he sucked on her clit, she let out a high-pitched cry he was sure they heard two apartments over and began to tremble. Determined to make her orgasm last as long as possible, he kept at her, licking and sucking, and that glorious sound filled his ears. Hands fisted around the comforter, Steph screamed her pleasure, belly and thighs shaking.

When she finally collapsed back on the bed and closed her legs, they were both panting. Gabe kissed his way back up her body. As he settled over her again, her thighs cradled his hips, but the heavy-lidded tenderness in her eyes caught him.

He lifted a hand, brushing the hair off her forehead with the tip of his finger as the emotion rolled around in his chest. He'd been attempting to deny it for years. The guilt it brought would crush him.

"I missed you, too." He prayed she understood, because he didn't have it in him to explain, wasn't sure he even wanted to dissect the feelings behind the words. She'd told him something similar on their first date, and he'd talked his way around it. Now he needed her to know that feeling hadn't been one-sided. For whatever the hell that was worth to her.

She didn't say anything. Instead, she lifted up and brushed a tender kiss across his mouth. He knew a stall tactic when he saw one. He was a master at distraction. So he leaned into her, allowed himself a moment to luxuriate in her soft lips tangling with his, then pulled back.

He caressed her bottom lip with his thumb. "Tell me what you're thinking. I can still see it, you know, when you're not telling me something. You get the same look on your face you used to get back then."

"It's nothing." She gave him a smile as phony as saccharine

and looked off to the left. The tension filling her body didn't escape his notice either.

He ducked his head and turned his mouth to her ear. "You do realize I can still tell when you're lying to me, right?" He nipped at the soft flesh of her earlobe. "Out with it."

When he pulled back again, her gaze searched his face. Finally, she blew out a heavy breath and closed her eyes. "It hurt when I stopped hearing from you. I've done the math, Gabe. Charlotte is ten, right? That means she was conceived about two months after you left."

Guilt tightened his chest. Damn. He'd always figured she had to feel that way. Betrayed. Hurt. He'd done exactly that—he'd dropped her like yesterday's underwear and moved on to the next woman.

He rolled onto his back beside her and held out an arm, but Steph didn't curl against him. Instead, she sat up and left the bed, striding toward the doorway. When she got there, however, she stopped, one hand on the frame.

"I'm not holding it against you. It was eleven years ago, and we've both changed in that time. But if you want me to pretend it didn't hurt or that I don't hesitate to spend more time with you, I can't do that. I told you. I wanted a weekend with a nice guy, and I'm grateful to you for that. I needed it, in ways I can't even begin to tell you. But I can't pretend I'm ready to just jump into this."

She didn't wait, but strode through the doorway and down the hallway.

Panic tightened in his chest, setting his heart hammering against his rib cage. Why did it feel like he was losing her all over again? If she walked out of his life, he couldn't say he'd blame her, but he'd just found her again. He had no desire to let her go yet.

"I thought about you a lot over the years." He raised his voice, calling out to her as he got out of bed and followed her. He hadn't a damn clue why he was telling her any of this. It likely wouldn't dissuade her. All he knew was he couldn't let her walk away without a fight. Not again. "When Char was born, I ached to call you. When I woke in the hospital, after I lost my leg, you were the first person I wanted to talk to."

The urge to share with her every triumph over the years had come strong. Eleven years and a lot of distance hadn't faded the need.

Rounding the hallway, he came to an abrupt halt. Steph stood outside the bathroom, one hand on the knob. When he came up behind her, stopping beyond her personal space, she folded her arms. "Yet you didn't."

Her tone was hard to read, and her stiff posture told him she wasn't giving him an inch. Clearly there was more to this than she'd let on.

Honesty. Right now he needed to be honest with her. In a way he should have been eleven years ago.

He blew out a heavy breath. "I didn't contact you because I wasn't sure you'd even want to hear from me anymore." When he'd left Seattle and gone home to Oregon, he hadn't handled their relationship with anything even resembling the respect and care she'd deserved. He'd been overwhelmed and had simply acted on instinct. One foot in front of the other. His parents' deaths had altered his whole life, throwing him into a loop that had taken him years to finally come to terms with.

He'd fucked up, plain and simple. All the sorry in the world didn't atone for it. All he could do now was explain and hope for the best.

"I never told Julia about us because our relationship started on shaky ground. Knowing about you would've hurt her, and I couldn't do that to her."

He'd missed Steph in ways a man married to another shouldn't. The guilt alone had eaten him alive. If he told her the truth, would she hold that against him or understand he'd never stopped caring about her?

"I just wanted you to know I thought about you. A lot."

She turned her head and stared at him, eyes reaching and searching. It wasn't the most romantic thing he'd ever told a woman before, but the admission was of the *heart on the sleeve* variety. He hadn't ever done that with anyone but her. Sadly, not even Julia.

Finally, her shoulders relaxed. "Thank you for being honest with me."

She didn't give him time to respond, but pivoted and moved into the bathroom, shutting the door behind her. He stared at the dark wood for a moment. He ought to leave now, let her have her space.

The pain twisting his gut into knots, however, wouldn't let him. Not like this. So, he returned to the bedroom and took a seat on the end of the bed. He'd let her have her space, but he wasn't letting this go that easily. He'd waited eleven years to clear the air with her. To tell her she'd meant more to him than a casual fuck. He needed her to know it, to believe it.

He shoved a shaky hand through his hair and glared at the opposite wall. He also wanted more time with her. Goddammit. Maybe even more than a casual fling, if he was really honest with himself. He hadn't expected to want to move on so soon, but he liked the way he felt when he was with her. Steph made him *want* to live, and he wanted to run with that feeling.

When Steph finally returned to the bedroom a few minutes later, she came up short in the doorway. "I thought you'd have left by now."

He pushed to his feet, slowly crossed the space, and stopped in front of her. He wanted to give her time to object, because if he pushed her too far, he had a feeling she'd bolt. "If you want me to leave, I will, but not until you tell me what you're thinking. We used to talk to each other, Steph. Stop shutting me out."

"What do you want me to say?" She shot him an irritated glance and moved around him to the dresser. There, she pulled open the top drawer, reached in, and came out with a pair of red silk panties. After stepping into them, she went into a lower drawer for a T-shirt, got one out and tugged it over her head. "It was eleven years ago. It's over."

He turned to watch as she climbed into bed. He wanted, ached, and needed to follow her, but clearly she didn't want him to, so he wouldn't push. At least, not tonight. "Then why do I get the feeling you're not telling me something?"

She slid beneath the sheets but kept her gaze on her lap, hands smoothing, restless, over the comforter. After a moment, her hands stilled, and she let out a heartfelt sigh, her shoulders rounding. "It's very disconcerting that you can still read me so well. You're right. I'm not. Maybe someday I'll share it with you, but I'm not comfortable doing it now."

His gut clenched. Damn. There was that wall again.

He crossed to the bed, took a seat, and picked up her right hand. Despite her stiff posture, she didn't pull it back, but neither would she look at him. She was putting up big walls against him, and he hated it with every fiber of his being. He'd seen that look on her face too damn many times. She used to give him similar ones in college, but he'd been too wrapped up in himself to figure out why.

"Give me a month, Steph. I won't make you any promises I can't keep, and you can uphold whatever boundaries you need. But I need you, and I think you want the same thing. Clearly I've hurt you, and I'd like a chance to make up for it." He stroked his fingers over her knuckles, heart in his throat. "For now I'll go. But this isn't over. Not by a long shot."

He leaned over, kissed her shoulder, and rose from the bed. He'd give her space, but one thing had become crystal clear. She didn't trust him.

He hated it. It ate away at his insides, because he couldn't help wondering. Was this stony wall because of him? Or because of that asshole who'd stood her up? Either way, he knew one thing right then: he'd earn her trust or die trying. Damned if he didn't want to be the one to prove to her that not all men were like her ex.

Despite her hesitations, she still responded to his touch. She was comfortable with sex. So that was where he'd start.

CHAPTER ELEVEN

The jingle of an incoming text jarred Steph awake. When she opened her eyes, the room around her sat cast in shadows. A glance at the clock on her nightstand confirmed it was after nine a.m., though the darkness of the room meant the spring sun had taken the day off. They were back to cold, wet, and miserable.

The quietness echoed around her. She reached out, smoothing a hand over the cool sheets beside her. Despite their conversation last night, she had to admit she missed him being there beside her. All of which meant she was already sliding down that slippery slope to falling in love with him again.

She heaved a sigh into the empty room. He had to go and play the good guy again, the knight in shining armor to her damsel in distress. One touch and she'd melted to his whim like ice cream on ninety-degree summer day.

Because she could resist him about as well as she could Lauren's chocolate-chocolate chip cookies.

When another text dinged in, she firmly set the thoughts aside and reached to the nightstand for her phone. She unlocked the screen and brought up her texts. While she hoped for a message from Lauren or Mandy, Gabe's name appeared twice.

Morning, baby. Car's done. All good. I can change your oil too but not today. Girls are rowdy.

Called Trent. Lauren should be there in an hour.

She blinked, rereading his words, then let her hand and the phone flop to the bed. How the hell was she supposed to keep him at a distance when he did things like this? Did he have any idea how normal he sounded? Like they were a couple and he'd texted to tell her he'd pick up milk on his way home from work.

Gabe Donovan was no longer that determined, cocky bachelor she'd known in college. He was a father, had been a lucky woman's husband. And that had changed everything. Resisting the man he'd become was a whole lot harder.

She stared at the textured ceiling above her, as if somehow it contained the answers she desperately needed. Hard as she tried to deny it, his sweet gesture tugged at her soft heart. Drew forth the silly romantic woman deep inside who wanted what Lauren and Trent had found. Who was tired of sleeping alone every night.

Before she'd had a chance to think about what on earth to say to him, another text popped up.

BTW . . . Friday. Dinner. My place. Not taking no for an answer.

She rolled her eyes, but shivers chased each other over the surface of her skin. He was sexy as hell in take-charge mode.

When he'd led her into the bedroom last night and peeled her dress off her, she'd lost the desire to send him home.

She drew a deep breath and punched in a quick reply.

And if I don't show up?

Thirty seconds or so passed before his reply came in.

Damn. I didn't realize you were there or I wouldn't have texted so much.

No more texting me, you. I'm not alone and you give me hard-ons.

She couldn't help the grin tugging at the corners of her mouth. Or the trip to her heartbeat. Damn him and his sexy sense of humor, too. Who in the world could say no to that? Certainly not her.

Before she could figure out how on earth to respond, another text popped in.

If you don't show up, I'll come get you. I have plans for you.

Plans? He'd made plans for *her*? Okay, she'd admit he'd piqued her curiosity. He was being pushy, but damned if it wasn't the sexiest thing any man had done for her in a long time. Simply because it made her feel wanted.

Gabe was a good man in all the ways that counted, and he wanted *her*. The crux of the matter was, she would never be anything more than a fling to him, a rebound. It was normal, natural, but how far gone would she be by the time the relationship reached its natural conclusion?

Another text came in before she had time to ponder a response.

I know you don't trust me, baby, but I can't fix it if you won't let me in. I won't deny I fucked up 11 years ago, but I'm not that guy anymore.

She stared at her phone. She *ought* to tell him it wasn't

because she didn't trust him. The pet name he called her, however, caught her, popping out from the screen, as if in bold, bright neon. *Baby*. Men called her that all the time, usually when they hoped to charm their way into her panties. From him, the cutesy name made her chest ache. She would never be his baby, but God how she wanted to be.

This time, when she responded, she had to be a little more honest.

Why is this so important to you? If sex is all you want, you could easily find a more willing date.

Thirty seconds passed before his reply came in, and Steph found herself holding her breath. She hated the thought of him with someone else. Always had. Including his wife.

Don't want just anybody. I WANT YOU.

Steph stared at the text, her heart hammering. The little devil on her shoulder poked her with his pitchfork. *You know damn well you want the same thing.*

No. She threw back the covers and dropped her legs over the side of the bed. This was one slippery slope she would not go down. It was time to pull out those boundaries. She was getting entirely too lost in him. Again. It stopped here, because she would not end up heartbroken when this ended.

Thanks for fixing the car. I owe you. I'll be over soon to pick it up.

She hit send on her reply, set her phone on the nightstand, and pushed to her feet. Moving to her dresser, she pulled out a pair of sweats, then grabbed her phone and headed into the kitchen. What she needed were huge quantities of coffee before Lauren got here.

Halfway to the kitchen, her phone dinged with the arrival of an incoming text. She made the mistake of glancing at the screen.

I look forward to it.

She groaned and moved to the coffeemaker. There went the whole morning. She'd spend it dreading seeing him. He'd toss her one of those sexy, flirty smiles and her panties would vaporize.

God help her when she actually arrived at his place. Her only hope at this point were those kids. With any luck, they'd provide enough of a distraction to keep her from giving in to temptation.

* * *

One cup of coffee and a quick shower later, Lauren had arrived, a small white bakery box in her hands. Standing out in the hallway, she lifted the box and smiled. "I come bearing goodies."

Steph clasped her hands together. "Please tell me they're those wonderful dark chocolate cookies..."

Lauren winked. "Would I have arrived with anything less?"

"Bless you. I so need chocolate this morning." Steph's stomach rumbled at the possibility. She took the box from Lauren and motioned her inside. "Come on in."

Lauren stepped across the threshold, closed the door, and followed as Steph made her way into the kitchen. "Man trouble? I expected Gabe to be here this morning, but Trent mentioned he'd called."

Steph's face heated as she set the box on the counter and glanced at Lauren. "I had plans to call you myself this morning, but he beat me to it. Coffee?"

Lauren pulled her lower lip into her mouth, nibbling on

the corner for a moment. "No, but thank you. No more coffee for me, at least . . . not for a while."

The hint in Lauren's voice had Steph pausing in the middle of reaching for the cabinet door. There were only a few reasons a woman would suddenly stop drinking coffee.

As the idea sank in, Steph spun to face her. "Oh my God. Are you . . . ?"

Lauren flushed to the roots of her dark hair and nodded. "I think so. I'm two weeks late, my breasts are tender, I'm tired all the time, and I've been getting nauseated."

Steph raised her brows. "You haven't done a test yet?"

Lauren gave a helpless shrug. "I kind of hoped you wouldn't mind stopping by the store on our way to pick up your car."

Steph would have squealed and clapped her hands in glee, but Lauren didn't look as excited as she might have expected her to. Her shifty gaze told Steph she was nervous.

"Of course." Steph enveloped Lauren in a hug, then pulled back, holding her by the upper arms. "So is this good news or bad? You look like you're about to puke."

Lauren waved a hand at her. "Oh, I'm just nervous. I thought I might be pregnant a few months ago. When it turned out to be a false alarm, Trent and I agreed we wanted to wait a while to have kids, enjoy being together, you know?"

Steph shook her head. "Don't be nervous. Even a blind fool can see that man's over the moon for you. He'll be thrilled." She picked up her purse off the counter, then grabbed Lauren's hand and headed for the front door. "Come on. There's a Walgreens around the corner."

Twenty minutes later, she and Lauren stood in her tiny bathroom. They were holding hands, staring down at the test stick on the counter. Poor Lauren was shaking like a leaf in the wind while they waited for the results.

Lauren jerked her gaze in Steph's direction, eyes wide and full of anxiety. "Distract me. Why isn't Gabe here?"

"Because he couldn't stay last night." She released a heavy breath. "I haven't decided yet if I'll take him up on his offer."

Lauren squeezed her fingers. "You're afraid."

"Not since my breakup with Alec have I spent this much time with the same man. I've only done one-night stands." Steph shook her head. "How did you do it?"

"I couldn't resist the chance to spend the time with Trent. I had no choice." Lauren turned her gaze to the test stick. "Oh God."

Steph followed Lauren's gaze. A faint plus sign appeared in the result window. Lauren sniffled, her eyes glistening with unshed tears.

Steph wrapped her in a fierce hug. "You're going to make a great mom."

Lauren pulled back, running her fingers beneath her eyes. "God I hope so."

"Taking care of people is what you do best. It's how you and Trent got together in the first place, right?"

Trent had been wounded in Iraq when an IED went off. He'd come home two years ago with PTSD and a heart full of survivor's guilt, determined to shut himself away from the world. He and Lauren had developed a friendship when she'd insisted on taking care of him. According to Mandy, Lauren had helped piece her brother back together.

Steph tossed Lauren a smile and winked. "Besides, how cool is it to have a mom whose job it is to make cookies and cupcakes all day?"

Lauren let out a breathy laugh and nodded in the direction of the front door, then turned and moved in that direction. "Come on. Let's go drop you off at Gabe's. I'm betting he's looking forward to seeing you."

Steph grabbed her purse off the counter and followed Lauren, her stomach suddenly lurching. "The problem is, I'm looking forward to seeing him, too."

They pulled up in front of Gabe's a half hour later to chaos. Out on the small front lawn, four little girls ran, screaming and giggling, in all directions. Gabe, looking delicious in a pair of well-fitted jeans and a T-shirt that hugged his glorious shoulders, lumbered along behind them. He hunkered down, arms outstretched, roaring and growling, to the delight of the girls.

He jogged up behind the smallest girl, a tiny brunette with the cutest little pigtails, and scooped her up. He hugged her to his chest and bent his head, his "nom, nom, nom" sounds carrying even through the closed car windows.

Steph dropped her head back against the seat, unable to help the hitch to her heart or stop her smile. "Gabe *demanded* dinner next Friday night."

"And you're going." Lauren looked over at her, brows furrowed, lips pursed, then reached for the door handle and inclined her head in the direction of the house. "Come on. Let's go say hello."

Steph drew a deep breath, summoned her professional side and the strength it lent her, and exited the car. The doors closing halted the action in the yard. Char and another, slightly smaller brunette skidded to a halt and turned to look. Gabe's head snapped in her direction. The instant his gaze hit hers, heat flared in his eyes, there and gone a breath later, but enough to set her insides on fire.

Her stomach did a triple looper. Steph halted on the sidewalk beside Lauren, every limb suddenly trembling. God. There it was. The look that would melt her defenses.

"And you're resisting that why?" Lauren leaned over, murmuring between them, then, just as suddenly, pulled away and stepped forward. "Morning, Gabe."

He set the girl on the ground and flashed a smile as he made his way in their direction. "Morning. Thanks for bringing her over, Lauren. As you can see, I've got my hands full today."

Lauren let out a quiet laugh. "It's no trouble at all."

Steph ignored the hitch to her heartbeat and followed Lauren onto the lawn. Coming to stand beside her, Steph smiled, praying it wasn't wobbling like her stomach. Did he have to look so delicious so early in the morning? "I appreciate you fixing the car."

He stuffed his fingertips in his pockets. "I told you. It's not a problem. I just appreciate you coming to get it. It's easier on my sanity than trapping these hooligans in a small, moving box." He chuckled, inclining in his head toward the girls, three of whom were now chasing each other around the yard. "I'm pretty sure Molly feeds them sugar for breakfast just to spite me."

"Well. I'll leave you to it. Seems I have a surprise to unleash on Trent." Lauren turned, eyes widening as she mouthed, *Call me!*

Fingers still casually tucked in his pockets, Gabe followed Lauren with his eyes as she returned to her car and climbed inside. "She's pregnant, isn't she?"

Steph raised her brows. "How in the world did you know?"

One shoulder hitched. "Julia and I tried for another child on and off. She lost a few. So I learned to recognize the symptoms after a while. Lauren came to the shop to have lunch with Trent last week. She couldn't stand the smell of the sandwiches she brought with her. In the half hour she was there, she took off running for the bathroom twice."

Her heart clenched, followed quickly by a twinge of guilt. She shouldn't allow it, but jealousy kicked her hard in the chest. He was still grieving his wife's death, but the knowledge seeped inside all the same.

"I'm sorry. That must have been very difficult for both of you." She pulled her shoulders back. She wasn't here to recount memories or indulge in that sexy sparring he was so damn good at. She'd come to get her car. "What do I owe you for the repairs?"

His head turned, his gaze settling on her. He studied her for a long, unnerving moment and reached out, then seemed to think better of it and stuffed the hand back in his pocket.

"I didn't tell you that to hurt you." She opened her mouth to protest, but he shook his head. "I can still read you, remember? I get it. There are things you don't want to tell me."

Feeling suddenly and overwhelmingly vulnerable, she folded her arms. It was the only barrier she had against him anymore. The more she saw him, the more she recognized the signs and the more it all came back.

When she didn't say anything, he continued. "I decided to be honest with you because I know I can't expect you to be honest with *me* if I'm not. I learned that lesson the hard way with Molly over the years. After Mom and Dad died, she resented me being her legal guardian and that I now had the power to tell her what to do. I learned if I was honest with her instead of just pushy and demanding, she didn't rebel quite so much."

Maybe he was right. Maybe it was time she was honest with *him*.

Careful to keep her voice low, she turned her head and looked off down the street. Honesty might be the best policy, but she couldn't force herself to look into that disarming hazel gaze while she said the words.

"I wasn't prepared for this. I was prepared for a weekend. A little fun with someone I trusted once. That's different, you know, than a hookup in a bar. But you're...you. It's childish, really, to still feel that way. To be jealous of a dead woman." She heaved a sigh and finally forced herself to look at him. "But I am."

Her insides shook as she waited. That was the most she'd ever told him. She didn't know if she actually wanted his response and yet part of her craved it. A holdover from all those years ago. Back in college, she'd wanted him to know she'd fallen in love with him, because she'd held out this hope he'd tell her he loved her back. Pathetic that the need still hovered beneath the surface.

Those keen eyes worked her face. Then, finally, he smiled, warm and alluring. "So, dinner? Next Friday?"

There was that sexy smile she'd known would make an

appearance, and she was caving, exactly the way she'd known she would.

She heaved a sigh and nodded. "Fine. You win. I'll have dinner with you next Friday. But since I owe you for the car and clearly you're not taking my money..."

"Nope." He winked, eyes gleaming with playful impishness and a touch of smug self-satisfaction.

Giddy, happy little butterflies took flight in her stomach. "Then I'm cooking."

One dark brow arched and the corners of his mouth twitched. "Can you do that?"

This time, her facade cracked. She punched him in the shoulder. "Yes, thank you very much. Contrary to popular belief, I have actually grown up."

Those gorgeous eyes glinted at her. "So you have."

"Friday. Six o'clock. Don't be late." She pivoted and marched toward her car, determined to get away from him before she embarrassed herself. As she reached into her purse, however, it hit her. Gabe had her keys. She halted, sighed, and, face hot as Hades itself, turned back.

Gabe stood grinning at her, his right arm extended. He jangled her keys, dangling from his thumb and forefinger. "Missing something?"

She rolled her eyes and strode back to him, but when she reached for the keys, he held tight to them.

"I look forward to seeing you, you know. I'll say it again, in case you missed my point last time. Were you anybody else, that first date wouldn't have gone this far." He finally released her keys and winked at her. "And I won't be late. I'm never late."

CHAPTER TWELVE

Friday night. Gabe blew out a nervous breath as he stood in the hallway outside Steph's apartment. He hadn't been this nervous about a date since junior high. More nervous even than his first day of BUD/S training. His stomach churned, and his hands shook so bad he feared he'd drop everything he'd carried from the car.

He was a SEAL for crying out loud. He'd moved into combat zones with less anxiety.

Music drifted through the closed door. A sultry pop song about love and sex if he heard the lyrics right. As he lifted his hand to knock, Steph's voice rose above the strains of music. She sang at the top of her lungs and completely off-key.

Steph, bless her heart, as his mother used to say, couldn't sing to save her life. He'd discovered the hard way one morning, back in college, that she loved to do it, too. Apparently, that hadn't changed either. She belted out the lyrics, her voice cracking as she hit a high note, but she kept right on going.

He winced, then chuckled and punched the doorbell.

The soft thump of her feet on the floor suggested she was on her way to answer. Seconds later, the door opened.

"Hi." She lifted a hand in greeting, but the smile she offered wobbled.

Some part of his brain told him to say something, but holy Christ, he couldn't move. Or blink for that matter. Steph had dressed to kill. Her burgundy top was skintight and cut low enough to tease him with mounds of creamy flesh above the neckline. The hem gave him a peek at her flat stomach. Her white skirt flounced around her thighs.

As he let his gaze drift over the length of her legs, the only thought in his head was bending her over the dining room table and flipping up that skirt. Was she wearing panties this time? God, he was dying to find out.

Gabe swallowed his tongue and finally managed to drag his gaze off her legs. "We are never making it to dinner."

"I take it that means you approve." She laughed, a sexy breathy sound that made her eyes dance and her nervousness seem to disappear.

He cocked a brow. "If I said no, would you take it all off?"

She rolled her eyes, and he could only laugh, feeling lighter than when he'd left the house. He hadn't planned a date with a woman in years, and his stomach roiled, but that sexy, flirty little smile she tried to hide made his nerves worth it. Whether or not this relationship went anywhere, he'd never be sorry he'd spent the time with her. Christ she made him glad to be alive.

She nodded at the stuff in his arms. "What's all that?"

"Ah." Right. He'd had plans when he'd come over here. He held out the box from the bakery first. "Dessert."

After accepting the box, she lifted the lid and peered inside. She smiled.

"Key lime pie." She looked up, her eyes gleaming with tenderness that made the effort suddenly worth it. "You remembered."

"I never forgot. You were lying in my arms late one night, and we were talking. You were telling me about your mom."

She nodded. "We were in your apartment, lying on that futon you had."

"Mm-hmm. You told me you had an affinity for key lime because your mother made the best pie."

She gave him a watery smile. "Nobody made it the way Mom did."

He held out the bottle of wine next. "I didn't know what you were serving, so I opted for white." Then he reached into the inside pocket of his jacket and pulled out the movie he'd picked up on his way over. "And this is for after dinner."

She quirked a brow. "A sci-fi movie?"

"Yup." He hoped she'd remember. B-rate sci-fi movies had always been their favorite. But that was okay. He'd have fun reminding her. He winked, then turned around and cocked his right hip at her. "Last but not least, these are for you."

Several unbearable seconds passed in silence as she stared at the tulips. He'd pulled out all the stops because he wanted to remind her how good they were together and to show her that, despite everything, he'd never forgotten her. Everything he'd brought with him had been inspired by memories of their time together. He prayed it worked. Her silence, though, made his nerves scatter.

Finally, she let out a heartfelt sigh and plucked the tulips from in his pocket.

"God, Gabe. They're beautiful."

The thoughtful edge to her voice made him turn back around. She stared at the bouquet, nose in the flowers. The tears hovering at the edges of her lashes told him where her thoughts had gone.

He stepped over the threshold. The soft scent of her perfume curled around his senses, begging him to bend his head to her neck, but he kept his hands to himself. He had every intention of providing enough temptation to melt even the coldest of hearts, but tonight he wanted the decision to be hers and hers alone.

"I know they're simple, but I chose tulips on purpose." He lifted a hand, fingering one of the long, thick leaves. "They planted rows of red ones outside your apartment back in college. It's funny. I never paid them much attention back then. But over the years, every time I'd see some, I'd think of you, of sneaking in through your back door at night, after class."

He could still see the building. Multicolored stucco in fall shades, the landscaping dotted with trees of various sizes and colors, and gardens full of brightly colored tulips. Steph had a first-floor apartment, and the flowers had lined either side of the little slab of cement that served as her back patio.

"Nobody's given me flowers in a long time." She looked up then, head tipped back, blue eyes studying his face. Then she laughed and dropped her forehead to his chest. "You are something else. She never stood a chance against you, did she?"

He didn't have to ask to understand she meant Julia and how long it had taken him to convince her to marry him.

"Nope, and neither do you." He settled his arm around her back and bent his head, kissing the top of hers. Several moments passed in comfortable silence. She didn't push him away, and he allowed himself the luxury of enjoying the feel of her against him. He turned his head and inhaled, but the smell of smoke hit his nostrils instead. He lifted his head, sniffing the air. "Babe, I think something's burning."

Her head snapped up, eyes wide. "Crap. The garlic bread!"

She pushed out of his arms, pivoted, and ran down the small hallway, disappearing around a corner. The clank of a metal pan hitting the top of the stove sounded seconds before an ear-piercing beep shrieked through the house.

He followed after her, leaving the door open behind him to air out the apartment. Coming to a halt in the kitchen entrance, he found Steph, towel in hand, waving it at the smoke alarm in the ceiling. The blackened remains of the garlic bread sat on a cookie sheet, still smoking. The tulips and dessert box lay, discarded, on the counter behind her.

She shot him a glare, her voice raised over the shrill of the alarm. "See what you do to me?"

He couldn't help the soft laugh that escaped him. Never in a million years would he tell her this, but he wasn't sorry he'd made her forget herself so completely she'd burned dinner.

He would, however, help her out. Reaching over her head, he unscrewed the alarm from its spot in the ceiling, then yanked out the battery. The deafening screech finally ceased.

Steph blew out a defeated breath, her shoulders rolling forward, and sagged back against the counter. "I am so not cut out for this domestic stuff."

He set the alarm on the counter, then moved to the sink

and opened the window to let the smoke out. When he turned again, she'd ducked her head into her hands and stood rubbing her temples.

Hoping to lighten the moment, he leaned beside her and bumped her shoulder. "Thought you said you could cook?"

She turned to glare at him again, but one corner of her mouth quirked upward. "No comments from the peanut gallery, thank you very much."

He hooked an arm around her shoulder, pulling her against his side.

"Relax. I'm teasing. It happens to the best of us. I've burned garlic bread before. And cupcakes I attempted for Char's birthday a couple years ago. And muffins she absolutely had to make one Saturday morning." He darted a sidelong glance at her, unable to hide his smile. "Which is how we know where that bakery around the corner is. Hell. I'm convinced the toaster has it out for me."

She let out a soft laugh. "Okay, you win."

He gave her shoulders a gentle rub, then moved to the stove, lifting the lid on the casserole dish seated there. Steam floated out, along with the luscious scent of fried eggplant and parmesan cheese. His stomach growled.

He darted a glance back at her. "Eggplant parmesan. I'm impressed."

"It was my mother's recipe. I haven't made it in years." She heaved a sigh and bumped the cookie sheet with her knuckles. "Would've gone better with garlic bread."

He leaned his mouth close to her ear. "Well, I'm starved. You either give me a plate, or I'm going to resort to eating you for dinner."

A soft flush rose into her cheeks. Steph released a serrated breath and turned to the flowers on the counter, gathering them with shaking hands.

"I need to put these in water first. You could get out plates if you like." She didn't wait for a response but turned and left the room, disappearing around the corner.

Gabe gritted his teeth and watched her go. He wanted her on edge, wanted her so hot she'd attack him before the night was over. But it had to be her choice, and if she was more comfortable taking it slow, he'd go at her pace. Which meant biding his time and playing the gentleman. Their first date with the agency, she'd had patience with him. The least he could do was give her the same courtesy.

He turned and searched the cabinets. By the time he found plates, she'd reentered the kitchen, vase in hand. They spent the next few minutes moving in silence, each tending to their tasks. The moment was painfully awkward yet oddly domestic. It reminded him too much of fights with Julia, when they'd gotten over being mad but still didn't know what to say to each other. With Steph the silence was...all wrong. As close as they'd gotten, they were light-years from where they'd been in college.

He moved to the cabinet he recalled having seen wineglasses in and pulled down two, set them on the counter beside her, then moved to the stove and began to portion out the dinner. He was reaching for a plate when she finally went still beside him.

"I can hear you thinking over there." Distracting himself, he scooped out a serving of the cheese-and tomato-sauce-covered eggplant.

"I'm sorry." She glanced over at him, face impassive, blue eyes searching, full of anxiety, and blew out a heavy breath. "This feels like a real date, and I'll admit I'm out of practice. I haven't done this in more than two years. You scare the hell out of me, Gabe."

"Good. You're not exactly a walk in the park for me either." He lightened his tone, aiming for a tease. If he didn't at least attempt humor, he'd be pinning her against this damn counter, hiking up that beautiful, pleated skirt, and burying himself to the hilt inside of her simply to feel her push back onto him. She might not be comfortable talking to him yet, but she responded to his touch, and damned if he didn't need that connection to her.

The fact of which scared the hell out of *him*.

Her facade finally cracked. She tossed a flirty, playful smile over her shoulder, eyes now glinting with impishness. "Are you telling me I'm difficult?"

"Learning to walk again was easier." He tossed a smile back at her, picked up the plates, and headed for the dining room, relieved the air between them had eased.

She followed moments later, setting a glass of wine at each spot. Standing beside him now, she laid a hand on his arm and peered up at him, expression somber but open. "Give me time."

He turned to her and cupped her cheeks in his hands, letting his thumbs stroke her supple skin. "I've got all the time in the world. How about we start simple? I won't make you any promises I can't keep if you stop shutting me out."

Her eyes widened, and she shook her head. "I'm——"

He covered her mouth with his, cutting off the rest of

whatever the hell she'd been about to say, and kissed her with all the frustration pent up inside of him. He wanted to possess her, to devour her. Just to feel her melt into him.

When she let out a maddening little whimper and leaned into him, he forced himself to release her. Breathing hard now, he furrowed his brow. "Apologize one more damn time and I'm going to fuck you on this counter."

To prove his point, he guided her fingers to the front placket of his jeans. He was harder than a steel rod. In two seconds flat, she had him shaking with need.

"Feel that? This is what you do to me. All I want right now is to bury myself inside of you, because Christ, Steph, I need that connection with you like I need to breathe. Or eat."

He released her hand and pivoted, paced away from her, dragging a hand through his hair as he moved. Frustration wound through his system, tying his gut in knots. His shoulders tightened to the point of aching. Self-loathing had a firm hold on his chest. They'd been so damn close once. Now she was a stranger, and he could blame only himself for it.

"You want to know why I let contact just drift off? Because I've always needed you this way. I didn't love Julia when I married her, but I respected her. I couldn't look her in the face and tell her you were just a friend, because I knew damn well you weren't. So I sacrificed our relationship to make my marriage work."

The truth sank over him, hard and heavy and cold, and his frustration flitted from his grasp as quickly as it started. He dropped his hand and blew out a defeated breath. He'd spent eleven years wishing he could have done things differently, kicking himself in the ass for the way he'd treated Steph in the end. Like she was nobody special. Wondering what might have happened if he'd had the balls to admit to himself that she'd meant more to him than just a good lay.

"I wasn't blowing smoke up your ass when I said I missed you." Standing now at the end of the table, staring at the outside lights seeping in through the miniblinds, he turned sideways and shot her a glare. "So you can run all you like, babe, but I'm not giving up on you. Not again."

The heavy emotion hanging over her finally lightened. Steph had the audacity to smile at him. Those blue eyes glinted with amusement as she sauntered over to him, lifted onto her toes, and brushed a tender kiss across his mouth. "And this is why you're my favorite boy toy."

He rolled his eyes, but damned if he could stop from smiling back at her. His irritation dissipated like wisps on a breeze, and the knots in his shoulders finally began to unravel.

Needing her close, he hooked her around the waist and tugged her against him. "I better be your *only* boy toy."

She rested her hands against his chest, palms searing his skin through his shirt. Her expression sobered. "You're a first for me. Since Alec, I mean. Despite what I told you on that first date, I've never actually spent a whole weekend with any one man. None of the guys I dated ever wanted to more one night."

He stroked her back, contenting himself with the feel of her in his arms. He was sure they'd made leaps and bounds tonight, in directions he didn't know if he was ready to go, but damned if he had the power to deny himself the luxury of following. "Does this mean you're giving me that month?"

She nodded and stroked her hands up his pecs to his

shoulders, her fingers gently caressing the back of his neck. "But you have to promise you'll be patient with me."

He leaned down, brushing a kiss across her mouth. "Ditto. How about we agree to meet once a week, on the weekends? I may not always be able to promise you the whole weekend, though. Single dad and all that. I'll have to talk to Molly, but I may only be able to swing a Friday or Saturday night. You okay with that?"

"I'm okay with that." Her hands stilled on his neck, and she stared for a moment, then lifted onto her toes, her mouth a hairbreadth from his. "Thank you."

"Not necessary. You did the same for me. Now we're even." He brushed another kiss across her mouth, then forced himself to release her. "Now feed me. Because that skirt you're wearing is driving me crazy, and if you don't keep me busy, I guarantee I'll misbehave."

She sauntered around the side of the table, ass swinging as she walked. "So it wouldn't be a good idea, then, to tell you I'm going commando tonight?"

He groaned. The vision in his mind was now complete. All he had to do was flip up that skirt and he could be inside her in less than a minute. If he tried hard enough, he could get her to come around him in less than five.

He pulled out his chair and dropped into the seat, darting a glance at her as he picked up his fork. "Remind me to bend you over my knee later."

As she slid into her seat, she tossed a saucy smile at him that lit him up from the inside out. "Sticks and stones, Gabe. Sticks and stones."

Gabe didn't have to ask to know what she meant. He knew

the words by heart. *Sticks and stones may break my bones, but whips and chains excite me.* It was the first time he'd made love to her, when their friendship had become...more. The night had started with their usual dinner and a movie on a Friday night. They'd been teasing each other when Steph tossed that doozy at him. They'd ended up naked five minutes later. To this day he couldn't remember the name of that movie, but he'd never forget her needy moan when he'd surged up into her. From that day on, she had only to whisper "stick and stones" in his ear to make him hard enough to hammer nails.

Which he was now.

Blood surging between his ears, he forced himself to fork a bite of food before answering. "Oh, you'll get yours, baby. You'll get yours."

CHAPTER THIRTEEN

Standing at the sink, Steph scrubbed stuck-on eggplant from a plate, a welcome distraction from her heated thoughts. Gabe had ambushed her. His gifts had been sweet. To know he'd thought about her over the years, that he hadn't just dropped her and moved on, had carved a chink out of her armor.

Dinner had been interesting. She and Gabe had made small talk, mostly chitchat consisting of "This is really good," and "Yeah, it turned out well." Gabe had gone a little *too* quiet over the course of the meal, but he'd tossed some steamy glances across the table. In the span of half an hour, he had everything below the belt throbbing. She had to resist the urge to press her thighs together for some relief.

Now he stood at the stove, putting the leftovers into a plastic container. Since she'd started cleaning the kitchen five minutes ago, he'd quietly helped, but he hovered beyond her peripherals. She couldn't tell if he was giving her space...or keeping his own. All the same, her senses homed in on him, following the sounds of his movements.

The fridge snapped shut, the sound almost a boom in the silence. When his soft footsteps headed in her direction, every muscle in her body tensed in anticipation of his touch. He didn't disappoint but pressed against her back, encompassing her in his warmth and the luscious strength of his body. Steph couldn't stop the blissful sigh that left her. His scent curled around her, masculine and clean and all Gabe.

A heady shiver shot down her spine, and her hands froze beneath the running water as she waited for his next move.

"I promised myself I'd behave. I had every intention of giving you time to adjust to this, to take this at *your* pace." His soft lips skimmed her shoulder as his big, warm hands caressed over the curve of her ass and down the backs of her thighs. "But I can't stand it. Knowing you're mine for the next month and that you aren't wearing panties beneath this skirt is driving me insane."

He continued his assault, sliding his hands beneath the hem of her skirt and lifting it. He pressed against her, pushing his erection into the cleft between her cheeks. They both groaned. Steph pushed back against him, legs already shaking, clit throbbing.

"Do you have any idea how much I want you right now?" His voice was a hot pulse against her neck as his soft lips skimmed her jaw, teeth lightly scraping her skin.

The second she'd agreed to spend an entire month with him, everything had changed. That fact alone seemed to have the wall she'd spent the last several weeks building against him crashing down around her. She hadn't a damn clue what happened next, but she knew one thing for certain: she'd never wanted another man the way she wanted him right then.

Instead of unzipping and pushing into her, though, he followed the curve of her ass with his warm hands. His long fingers dipped between her thighs to graze her center, and a needy moan slid out of her. In reaction to his silent question, she pressed her ass into his hands.

His quiet chuckle rumbled against her throat. "Is that a yes?"

Desperate now to feel all of him, she pushed back harder into the ridge of his erection, and one calloused fingertip grazed her aching clit. Pleasure exploded along sensitive nerve endings, and she moaned again. God, he was the only man who did this to her, who made her lose herself in his touch.

"Yes." She rocked her hips, riding that luscious finger, trying to quench the unbelievable hunger he sent spiraling through her. "God, yes."

He held himself just out of reach, his finger grazing everything but connecting with nothing. Frustration wound through her system. She pushed back harder, widened her stance, and offered herself to him. When he finally obliged and slid that wicked finger inside, Steph let out a needy, desperate moan.

Gabe groaned against her throat. "Say my name, baby. Christ, I love it when you moan my name."

Shaking all over now, breaths coming in erratic pants, she let her head fall forward in abandon. "Gabe..."

He pushed that finger in deeper and found a rhythm, sliding all the way in, pulling all the way out, only to push back in with the same agonizing slowness. He ramped up her yearning to a frenzy, fanning the sweet fire within. All the while his mouth skimmed the skin of her neck and his other hand curved around her left breast, fingers pinching the tightened nipple. "Tell me what you want, Steph."

"You. I need *you*." She groped behind her, reaching for any part of him she could get a hand on, but only managed to connect with his hip. "Gabe, please."

He pulled his finger from her. His body shook against her back, his breaths soughing against her skin. "Jesus. I can't stand it. I wanted to tease, to make you come, but, Christ, when you say my name like that..."

He fumbled behind her, and the rasp of a zipper sounded in the silence. Every inch of her trembled with anticipation, and Steph widened her stance, just the promise of him sliding into her enough to loosen her joints.

Seconds later he gripped her hips and pushed into her in one long, slow wet stroke. Pleasure erupted along her nerve endings. A wildfire seeped along her skin. Steph let out a long, shuddering breath.

Gabe bent over her back, pressed his cheek to hers, his breaths harsh against her ear. One hand splayed over her left hip, holding her firmly to him. The other hand braced against the counter's edge as he began a punishing rhythm, pushing into her to the hilt so hard all the breath left her lungs. Every hard thrust jarred through her, ramping up the unbelievable pleasure.

She gripped the sink's edge and pushed back. She needed this as much as he did.

The sound of flesh slapping flesh filled the room around them. His groans mixed with the soft cries she couldn't contain. He'd struck a match and lit her whole body on fire. His thick cock rubbed all the right places inside, and every stroke sent her careening toward oblivion so quickly she couldn't catch her breath.

Another quick, hard thrust and a shower of pleasure erupted along her nerve endings. The dam inside of her burst, her orgasm tearing through her.

"Gabe..." She curled her fingers around the edge of the counter until her nails hurt, shaking and panting, her hips bucking against him as she rode that luscious wave.

Seconds later he swore softly in her ear, then let out a low groan. His thrusts grew a jerky hitch, slowing as he found his own release deep inside of her.

Like a marionette with his strings cut, he went limp, his body warm and deliciously heavy against her back. Steph blew out her held breath. Long moments passed before either of them did much more than tremble quietly together, both gulping in deep lungfuls of air.

Gabe moved first. He straightened, pulling her up with him, but didn't step back. Instead, his arms banded around her waist, drawing her back against him.

"We're going to kill each other before this month is over." His voice was a husky rumble, still breathless but full of amusement. "I'm going to die of exhaustion."

She let her head fall back against his shoulder. "Is there a better way to go?"

"Than buried deep inside of you?" He ducked his head, his voice a husky rumble against her throat as he skimmed his mouth up the side of her neck. "Nope."

She slid her hands along his arms, fingers skimming the downy hairs. Gabe continued to nuzzle her neck and her ear, and Steph couldn't bring herself to break the intimate connection. The sweet lull of satiated fatigue made her limbs deliciously heavy, but she rode a high nothing could touch. Her heart would end up broken at the end of this month—of that she was now certain—but she couldn't bring herself to care. She couldn't stay away from him if she tried.

Lauren was right. Gabe was exactly what she needed, and when it was all said and done, she'd walk away with memories she'd treasure.

He turned his head, his nose nudging her earlobe, then let out a heavy sigh. "We forgot the condom, babe."

She peered over her shoulder as far as their position would allow. Given how his marriage had started, she couldn't blame him for worrying. She wasn't ready to be a parent yet, and getting pregnant would be a complication neither of them needed.

"It's okay. Condoms are always safer, but I'm on the pill." She shrugged. "Have been for a while now."

He turned his head, his voice a husky murmur against her throat. "Just remember, you're mine for the next month."

His quiet statement landed its punch . . . right in her heart. With any other man, that possessiveness would have pissed her off. Steph Mason belonged to no man. She'd worked damn hard to maintain her freedom.

Coming from him, however, it made her chest ache. He had no idea exactly how much she was *already* his.

She pulled away, a soft shiver moving through her as he slipped out of her. Then she turned in his arms and brushed a kiss across his mouth. "I'll be right back. I need to go clean up."

He nodded, and she moved around him, heading for the

bathroom around the corner. By the time she returned, he had his pants fixed and stood leaning back against the counter. Hands trembling with nerves, she came to a stop in front of him. She drew a deep breath, gathering her courage.

"For the record, I'm not seeing anybody else, nor do I plan to." She dropped her gaze to his chest, vulnerability moving over her. He needed to hear the truth, and some part of her *wanted* him to know. She needed the intimate connection sharing with him would give her. Neither could she look him in the eye when she said the words. "Truth is, I haven't seen anybody in a while."

She hadn't gone clubbing in months, at least not with the intention of picking up a date. The desire had worn thin. Now here was Gabe. Once their fling ended, she suspected it would be a while before she'd *want* to see anyone else. How the heck could she possibly top him? She'd be left empty and bereft for the umpteenth time in her life, but she could never regret this time with him.

Then and there the decision made itself. For this month, she'd allow herself to enjoy being with him and damn the consequences to her heart.

So she lifted her gaze, offered him a soft smile, and closed the distance between them. She leaned into him and slid her hands up his back, gathering him closer. "I'm yours, Gabe."

His hands slid to her ass, holding her loosely, as if somehow they belonged there. He dropped his forehead to hers. "Good."

"So you'll stay?" Yeah, she was wearing heart on her sleeve with this one, but she needed him to stay, to spend the night wrapped in his embrace. He made her feel sheltered. Adored.

More than she could possibly tell him. She was tired of sleeping alone, and he was everything her soul craved.

His forehead rocked against hers as he nodded. "I'll stay. I'll need to go get my crutches from the car, though."

He'd brought his crutches with him. From their weekend together, she knew Gabe took his prosthetic off at night, using his crutches until he got up in the morning. If he'd brought his crutches with him, it meant he'd already planned to spend the night. That fact awed her. That, along with the gifts he'd brought, had a foreign emotion curling through her chest. It felt an awful lot like admiration and joy and bliss. Which was about two steps from love.

She stood firmly on the nose of a sinking ship.

"Showering will be tough. I'm afraid I don't have a seat in mine." She rubbed a hand over his chest, her stomach clenching. Her tiny little apartment wasn't anything he needed, but it meant the world to her that he'd stay anyway. And she hadn't a damn clue how to tell him that.

She looked up at him, more open and exposed than she'd been in a long damn time, and gave a helpless, apologetic shrug.

He lifted a hand, thumb gently sweeping her chin, voice quiet and gentle. "It's okay. We'll figure it out."

She smiled again, relieved, and nodded, then slid her hands up his back, gathering him closer. "So, what now? What was in your arsenal for tonight?"

He cocked an amused brow, eyes glimmering with playful impishness. "Since you waylaid my plans tonight..."

She dropped her gaze to his chest, her cheeks heating. "I hadn't intended to. I'd intended to hold out."

His hands stroked her back, slow and somehow reassuring. "So why did you?"

She shrugged. "I talked to Lauren. She and Trent did something similar, and she told me she didn't regret her time with him." She peeked up at him, one corner of her mouth hitching. "And then you show up with all this stuff. Not a single man in the last two years has gone through that much trouble for me. What woman in her right mind could resist?"

Amusement glinted in his eyes. "It's a good thing I found you, then. You were spending time with all the wrong kinds of men."

She let out a quiet laugh. "*There's* that cocky guy I know. Thought maybe you'd gone soft over the years."

"Not a chance." He leaned down, caught her bottom lip in his teeth and tugged gently. "Shall we go watch a movie?"

She nodded, offering him a soft smile. "I'd love to."

It was so simple and something they might have done eleven years ago, enjoyed spending time together. Having spent eleven years apart, the time seemed all the more finite and that much more...precious.

He stepped back and offered his hand, then led her into the living room and took a seat. As she settled onto the couch beside him, he looked over at her and lifted his arm. The vulnerability in his gaze, the bare need, had her scooting over. As she snuggled against his side, tucking her forehead into the crook of his neck, the bliss settled over her.

Feet tucked up on the couch beside her, she wrapped an arm over his belly. "I've really missed this, Gabe."

She was one hundred percent immersed in and surrounded by him. And she had no desire to be anywhere else.

He pressed a tender kiss to the top of her head, murmuring into her hair, "Me too."

* * *

Steph came awake the next morning to tangled limbs and a luscious, warm, male body tucked against her side. She opened her eyes slowly, blinking against the bright sunlight that flooded the room. Her gaze landed on Gabe. He lay facing her, eyes closed, mouth slack in peaceful slumber.

She couldn't help the hitch to her heart. She'd slept wrapped in his embrace, peaceful and content for the first time in years. Oddly enough, they hadn't made love again last night. She'd fallen asleep in her pj's, him in his boxers, tucked against the warmth and solidity of his big body. She couldn't remember the last time she'd felt that close to a man. Certainly not Alec.

Gabe seemed to feel the intimacy between them as well. He'd stayed by her side all night. The beefy arm currently flung over her belly had remained there. He'd made sure of it. She'd woken more than once last night when, having drifted away from her during their sleep, he snagged her side and tugged her back against him. Though she couldn't be sure whether he was conscious of it or if it was something he'd done instinctively.

Not that she cared.

She reached up, tracing his features with her fingertip. Over his dark brows. Down his long nose. Along his full bottom lip. For the next three weeks, she could pretend she was his and he was hers. When it ended, she had no idea what would become of their relationship. Would they even stay friends? Or would they go their separate ways again?

The thought brought with it a heartbreaking new question. Namely, how would she handle being only his friend, knowing she loved him?

Because she did. Lying there with him, watching him sleep, her heart swelled and ached at the same time. She couldn't deny it anymore. She'd always loved him. Nothing had changed in that respect. And she loved the man he'd become. He was the stuff dreams were made of.

She pressed a kiss to his forehead, then carefully slid out from beneath his arm and crept from the bed. After a quick trip to the bathroom, she made her way to the kitchen. Ten minutes later, when Gabe came around the corner, dressed only in his jeans, the coffee began to sputter into the pot, filling the kitchen with its rich aroma.

"Morning." She tossed him a smile and turned to lean back against the counter, watching as he shuffled, eyes still half closed, across the kitchen to her.

He slid his hands onto her hips, and leaned into her. His scent and the warmth of his body enveloped her as he bent his head, nose skimming the side of her neck. "Woke without you."

The deep gravelly rumble of his voice sent hot little shivers chasing one another over the surface of her skin. His soft lips moved, skimming across her shoulder and up her neck. His hips shifted, rocked into her, and his erection pressed into her belly.

Her breathing hitched, and just that fast, her head fell back on a shuddering breath. God, he was potent like this, turned on and taking what he wanted. She could barely get her tongue to form words. "Sorry. I... wanted to let you sleep."

He growled low in his throat, a sound of frustrated, aroused male, and his teeth closed gently over her earlobe. "Would've rather you'd woken me up."

Her hands automatically reached for him, sliding up his back. God, he was still warm, too, skin luxuriously smooth. Apparently not done tormenting her, those big hands burrowed beneath the T-shirt she'd donned before bed last night, slid over her hips and straight into the back of her panties. He cupped her ass, dragging her hard against him, then pushed her panties down.

The satin dropped to her feet with a swish of fabric, then Gabe cupped her ass and lifted. He set her on the counter and edged between her thighs. They were face-to-face now, his mouth a scant inch from hers, his warm breaths fanning her skin. Electricity arced between them. "Know what I missed the most about you?"

Her heart skipped a beat. She was afraid to ask. Almost.

Breathing harsh and erratic, she forced herself to hold his gaze. "What's that?"

"Being able to do this..." He bent his head again, his lips brushing hers. The tenderness of the touch contradicted the take-charge mood he seemed to be in, and a soft, shuddering breath left her. "Whenever I feel like it. Just *because* I feel like it."

His lips brushed hers again. Once. Twice. Then he covered her mouth with his. What started as a tease became an erotic yet incredibly tender play of lips. He didn't seem in much of a hurry, but sipped and tasted like he had all the time in the world.

Except his hands hadn't stopped moving. They caressed up her thighs. His thumbs grazed her heat, enough to light a fire in her belly, only to skirt away, leaving her panting and squirming on the counter. Warm, work-roughened skin provided a delicious contrast of sensation as those hands skimmed over her hips and tugged her to the edge of the counter. His erection now settled exactly where she wanted him, only his jeans separating them. Her clit lit up as surely as if he'd stroked her with his oh-so-talented tongue.

"For the next month, you're mine, and I can take you whenever I want you."

The possessiveness in his tone made her throb with almost painful pleasure. Her hands curled around the nape of his neck, holding on for dear life. Steph gave up any semblance of protest and let her head fall back in abandon. She couldn't stop the blasted tremors. So turned on, she couldn't think properly, and her tongue refused to cooperate.

"Do you w-want me now?" She needed to hear him say the words. He had a penchant for telling her exactly what he wanted seconds before he took it. It was so goddamn sexy. She needed those words more than the coffee she'd just brewed.

Using his purchase on her ass, he pulled her the tiniest bit closer, rocking his erection against her heat, and flicked his tongue against her sensitive earlobe. "You tell me."

Her clit throbbed in eager anticipation, and a quiet moan escaped her. She rocked her hips into him, fingernails digging into his skin with the combination of frustration and need winding through her. "Say the words, Gabe. I need to hear the words."

His hands released her. Seconds later the rasp of a zipper sounded in the silence.

Steph shivered in anticipation.

His hands regained their hold on her hips as his hot mouth skimmed her throat. The tip of his cock pressed at her entrance, but he didn't push forward. Instead, his voice came warm and husky in her ear. "You. I want to bury myself so damn deep inside of you you'll be feeling me there for weeks. I want to feel your body clamp around my cock and your hips push into mine because you can't help yourself. But you know what I want the most, baby?"

Heat prickled over the surface of her skin. "What's that?"

"I want to hear you moan my name when you come." Hands gripping her hips, he surged forward, sliding into her in one delicious quick thrust.

Her body bowed into the intense connection, her hips pushing into his. *"Ohhh!"*

She wasn't sure if he meant to stake his claim by taking her that way, or if he was just as lost in the need as she was, but right then she *felt* wholly claimed.

When he didn't move but seemed to sit there for a moment, reminiscent of the first time they'd made love, she groaned in frustration.

"Gabe, please. I need you to move." She thrust against him as much as the position would allow. His cock slid deeper by only a fraction, but nudged a sweet spot inside, and her thighs fell open on a quiet, needy moan. "Oh God, please."

He turned his head, mouth skimming over hers. "I'm sorry. You just feel so fucking incredible."

He finally began to move, but once again seemed to be taking it as his own pace. She'd expected hard and fast. Despite the tension straining the muscles of his arms and shoulders, he moved slow and steady. Sliding inch by inch all the way out. Pushing back in the same way.

"I just want to stay here."

The awe in his voice had the same emotion moving over her. His scent filled her lungs with every desperate gasp of air she managed to drag in as he filled her, retreated, filled her again. Never once did his gaze shift from her.

That hot gaze rooted her, caught her like a fly in a spiderweb, and sucked her in. Until she took every breath with him, watched his pleasure and let it fuel her own. It was delicious and torturous and the most intimacy she'd ever shared with one person. She wanted to wrap herself around him and somehow take him deeper, to climb inside of him.

Her orgasm hit out of nowhere, a bone-melting rush of pleasure that flooded every cell. Her eyes slammed shut and a choked cry escaped her. "Gabe!"

"Fuck."

Gabe's quiet curse came seconds later. His fingers dug almost painfully into her skin as his body shook against her, his hips jerking as he emptied himself deep inside of her.

When the spasms finally ended, his arms banded around her back, crushing her to him, and he dropped his forehead onto her shoulder. His breaths sawed in and out of his mouth, hot against her neck.

Her chest squeezed and tears she couldn't begin to explain

or even understand pricked at her eyes. She hadn't made love to a man since Alec. Oh, she'd been with enough men to know the difference. The connection to Gabe was intense. She'd wanted the whole cliché, to be so close they fused.

She turned her head and buried her face in his throat, let his scent wash over her and calm the choking haze of panic gripping her in a vise.

Something Gabe must have caught, for his hands stroked her back, gentle and soothing. He pressed a soft kiss to the side of her neck, murmuring against her skin, "You okay?"

"No." She tightened her hold on his shoulders and burrowed deeper into his neck. "Don't let go. Please. Not yet."

Gabe stiffened against her and went so still his thoughts hung heavy in the air. She couldn't decide if she wanted him to voice them or keep them to himself. Things had clearly changed between them. They hadn't needed each other quite this much before.

In three weeks, she'd have to let him go. It was all she'd thought about while lying in bed beside him last night. Despite the closeness that had developed between them, Gabe's heart was still under lock and key. He would never really be hers.

All of which meant she had a difficult decision on her plate. When their time together ended, could she let him walk away from her again? Or take him as he was?

CHAPTER FOURTEEN

The following morning Gabe lay in the dark, staring at the shadowy ceiling above him, his hands roaming the curves of Steph's body. She lay naked on his chest, her skin warm and soft. They'd been lying there for some time now, nothing between them but the moonlight streaming in through the window.

She'd come over for dinner last night. He'd ordered take-out, Chinese this time, and although he'd rented a movie, they hadn't made it that far. Like the previous weekend, they'd ended up naked and wrapped around each other. Dessert had taken an erotic twist, and one thing had led to another.

He couldn't sleep, as usual, and the restlessness of her fingers over his belly told him she wasn't asleep either. Yet despite them being as close as two people could get, she'd gone a little *too* quiet. She'd always been the talker of the two of them, so when she went quiet, he'd always known it meant she was pondering big things. He had a feeling she was making some sort of decision, and the thought of the outcome had anxiousness caging his chest.

Since their lovemaking in the kitchen yesterday, something had changed between them. He'd needed her then, to hold her, to connect to her, on the most primal level. For the first time in months, his nightmares had returned. Sleeping in an unfamiliar place had apparently disoriented his senses. Steph's warm body in the bed beside him, though, had calmed the choking haze of grief and panic he'd woken with.

Christ, he couldn't remember the last time he'd felt this close to someone. Like they were one soul. It was a walking fucking cliché, but he could see it in Steph's eyes, feel the power in her tender touch, in the way her body curled into his. She didn't just hold him; she clung to him. Even now her body might as well have been a second skin.

Her silence had his mind going in too many damn directions.

"I can feel you thinking up there." He lifted his head and pressed a kiss to the curve of her shoulder. "Don't shut me out."

Seconds ticked out in more unbearable silence, and his gut twisted. Would she even tell him? Had he pushed her too far? He hated the thought, but he couldn't fix what was wrong if she wouldn't talk to him.

After a few moments, she slid into the space beside him and laid her head on his shoulder. "Last weekend I told you there was something I wasn't telling you. Do you remember?"

He couldn't forget. There'd been too much distance between them then, too.

He wrapped his arm around her back, stroking his fingers

along her spine. "Does this mean you feel comfortable telling me now?"

"Not entirely, no, but I need you to know. It's my one regret." Her hand slid over his belly, her slender fingers sifting through the hairs there in an idle fashion. "I loved you back then. That's what I didn't tell you, and why, sometimes, I can be so distant. You were the first man I really loved and the first man to really hurt me. So you're both ends of the same spectrum for me, Gabe. Good and bad, pain and bliss."

His chest squeezed, a sick sensation churning up his gut, and a million more questions popped up right behind it. He'd always known he'd hurt her, leaving the way he had, but he'd never realized to what degree.

He reached up, stroking her cheek with his fingers in an attempt to soothe, to connect. "Why didn't you ever tell me?"

She let out a short bark of laughter. "Because I knew you didn't feel the same way. You were very driven by your career, and I knew I was only a stop along the way. Back then it was enough." One shoulder hitched, and her voice lowered to a husky murmur. "I missed you when you left, though."

He wanted to ask if what they had now was enough. Or something like it. A next step. For the first time since Julia's death, Steph had him pondering the possibility of more than just weekends full of great sex. A real relationship even. He wasn't sure he was ready for much more than that yet, though. The forever part. And Steph was, even if she was too scared to go after it. She'd all but told him that on their first date. She might not want to get hurt again, but Steph was a permanent kind of girl.

Instead, needing and craving that connection to her, he

reached between them and curled his hand around hers. "So why tell me now?"

"Because I need you to know." She tilted her chin and peered up at him, watching him with careful eyes for a moment. "I know I promised you a month, but I'm not sure how much longer I can do this with you."

Suspicion itched at the edge of consciousness. "What aren't you telling me, Steph?"

She let out a heavy sigh and rolled over, turned her back to him, and tucked a hand beneath her pillow. "It doesn't matter. I'm a rebound for you, Gabe. There's only one way this ends."

For a moment all he could do was stare at the shape of her body and process. Steph's words echoed in his head like that old record player his mother'd had when he was little. *I loved you.* His stomach twisted, guilt rising like a typhoon over his head. He'd been deluding himself to think they could simply enjoy each other in the here and now and worry about the forever part later.

That he could get back those years they'd lost, like it was nothing.

It would never be uncomplicated with her, because she wasn't just *any* woman. She'd been his best friend once, and she cared. She was right. She needed and deserved a man who could whisper those three little words back to her, and he couldn't be that man. At least not yet. Oh, he wanted to be. God, how he ached to be. Maybe someday he'd get there, but asking her to wait, to hang her hopes on something that might not happen, was selfish at best.

He'd hurt her enough.

He snuggled up against her back and wrapped an arm

around her, tucking her securely against him. When she didn't push him away or stiffen, relief flooded his chest. Their relationship suddenly seemed more finite, and it scared the hell out of him. He had a feeling he was going to have to let her go, and the thought alone had a sick sensation twisting up his stomach. He was losing her. Again.

He pressed a kiss to the back of her neck. "I never meant to hurt you. You have to know that."

Her hand slid along his arm, soft, slender fingers finding his where they rested at her waist. "I know."

He blew out the breath he'd been holding. He didn't deserve her forgiveness, but it went a long way to easing his conscience.

"I don't blame you for wanting to end this, for whatever the hell that's worth. I need you. I can't begin to tell you how much. And not just anybody. You. But it's a profoundly selfish need." He tightened his arm around her waist and pressed a kiss to the back of her shoulder as if somehow that would make up for the pain he'd caused her eleven years ago. "You deserve the forever guy, Steph, and right now I don't know if I can be the man you need. Not yet."

He was ready to move on with his life, but to let himself fall in love? With Steph? His entire marriage to Julia, he hadn't forgotten or stopped thinking about or missing Steph. It'd had him questioning his marriage, hell, questioning himself. What kind of husband still missed an ex-lover? What kind of person did that make him?

"I also have Char to think about in all of this. If she gets attached, she ends up a casualty." He ached to somehow soothe the wound he'd clearly created, but what the hell could he do? Steph deserved complete honesty, and it was about time he gave it to her. Even if the thought of never seeing her again made his chest want to cave in.

She released his hand and rolled back to face him, lying so close their noses practically touched and her soft, minty breaths puffed against his lips. "Thank you for being honest with me. For what it's worth? I don't regret the time with you. You were exactly what I needed. You restored my faith in the male population."

"Glad I could be of service." He forced a laugh, praying it didn't sound as false as it felt. He appreciated the sentiment, but right then laughing was the last thing he felt like doing.

Her echo of laughter faded as quickly as it came, and silence once again moved over them, growing heavy with all the things they weren't saying to each other. A vise had a permanent hold on his chest, and his gut churned with a mixture of regret and sadness and a need impossible to fulfill.

He rolled onto his back and lifted an arm. Steph snuggled up to his side, once again resting her head on his shoulder. Her hand settled, warm and heavy, on his stomach. For a moment they lay in silence, this time comfortable but aching. He turned his head, pressed his nose into her hair, and inhaled, breathing her in. His lungs filled with the soft scent of her perfume combined with the clean aroma of her shampoo. He wanted to remember that scent to get him through the lonely nights to come.

He tightened his hold on her, his chest threatening to cave in. He had to let her go. Again. Only this time she was the one walking away. "So what now?"

Her body tensed against his side. Several seconds ticked,

the air between them no longer relaxed and intimate but tense and too damn quiet. Once again they were strangers, and he fucking hated it.

Finally, she tucked her forehead into his neck. "I'll leave in the morning."

Relief shuddered through him. He'd never been gladder to hear those words. He still had to give her up, but at least it wouldn't be tonight. The finality of the moment settled over him, leaving him cold. History, it seemed, really was doomed to repeat itself.

"Gabe?"

Her voice came as quiet as the night around them, a bare murmur in the darkness. He turned his head toward hers, stroked her back, soaking in the feel of her against him. "Hmm?"

She rubbed a hand slowly over his belly, gentle and soothing. "Thank you. For understanding, I mean."

"I'll be honest, Steph. I hate the thought of not seeing you again, but I want you to be happy."

He also hated the idea of her with someone else, but he kept that thought to himself. She didn't need to hear it. It also wouldn't serve any purpose except to make them both feel worse than they already did. Who'd have thought a simple fling could lead them here?

He pressed a kiss into her hair. "Like I said, I can't ask you to wait. I think you deserve better."

* * *

Gabe woke the following morning to an eerily silent house. Light filtered in through the sheer curtains on the bedroom window, filling the room with a play of sunlight and shadow. Outside, dozens of noisy, happy birds had what sounded like a conversation, chirping back and forth to each other.

As he blinked up at the ceiling, the deafening quiet slid over him, sinking inside him. Instinct told him Steph had left sometime in the early morning. He turned his head, staring at the empty pillow beside him. Only his memories and the indent her head had made told him she'd ever been there. Sliding his hand over the sheets, he found them cold as well.

He closed his eyes against the chest-crushing ache, allowed himself a moment to wallow in self-pity, then forced himself to release the heavy emotions and opened his eyes. What he needed was to get back into his weekend routine. Keep himself busy.

So he sat up and, after pulling on his shorts, reached for his crutches and got out of bed. He usually took off the prosthesis after dinner each night, using his crutches until after he had his shower the next morning. It was just easier, and it gave his leg a break. Now it would be part of the routine, and this morning he desperately needed it.

He and Steph had made love all night. He'd taken his time, savored every inch of her. He'd burned every moment with her into his memory. The scent of her skin. The tremor in her voice when she cried out. The luscious sound of her laugh, deep and throaty and honest. Even the simple luxury of sitting with her at the breakfast bar and chatting over a late-night cup of coffee.

He wouldn't get that luxury this morning, and the knowledge sat hard and heavy inside of him.

As he rounded the corner, heading into the kitchen, a piece of paper on the counter stopped him cold. It sat in front of the first seat at the breakfast bar, folded in half, with his name neatly scrawled across it in smooth, flowing handwriting.

For a moment he could only stare at the page, his heart hammering in his ears. The need to pick it up, for that one last connection to her, hit him with all the force of a meaty fist to the gut, knocking the breath from his lungs.

He turned instead and made his way to the coffeemaker. He emptied yesterday's contents and set a new pot to brew before forcing himself to face that note. The paper shook in his hand when he finally plucked it off the counter and opened it.

I'm sorry I didn't wake you. I didn't have it in me to say goodbye to you one more time. It just would have been too hard. Take care of yourself, Gabe. I have no regrets.

~Steph

As he stared at her words, processing slowly the moment he'd arrived at, that familiar ache settled in its place inside of him. He was alone. Again. His life would go back its new normal. He'd bury himself in work during the day and Char in the evenings and weekends. Every night he'd try to sleep while lying in bed pondering the fucking ceiling.

He tried to convince himself he didn't feel broken, that loneliness wasn't eating a hole in his chest. He'd never again get to see Steph's bright smile or hear her addicting giggle. Or fall asleep wrapped in the softness of her embrace. She'd go back to seeing other men, would move on with her life, none of which included him.

And he had to let her do it, because what the hell could he offer her? A handful of promises?

He swore under his breath, wadded the note, and hurled the paper ball in the direction of the living room with all the frustration winding through him. It sailed over the island and dropped somewhere on the other side. His shoulders tensed to the point of pain, and Gabe pivoted, dragging both hands through his hair.

He fucking hated this place in his life. He'd been here for too damn long, living somewhere between regret and grief. First when Julia died and now with Steph's departure from his life. He'd hated letting her go the first time and despised it even more now. It was like watching the never-ending cloud cover close off that tiny, brilliant gift of sun, leaving him once again in depressing shades of gray.

And he missed her. Goddamn it.

CHAPTER FIFTEEN

Steph pushed off her couch, taking her wineglass with her as she paced out into the middle of the living room. She stared on the TV, several feet in front of her. The images playing on the screen blurred as her gaze unfocused. Lauren and Mandy sat on the sofa behind her, waiting for her response to a question she didn't know how to answer.

"Why aren't you with Gabe?"

Lauren had asked her that an hour ago when she and Mandy had arrived. Not wanting to spend the evening alone and entirely too aware she wouldn't be spending this weekend with Gabe, she'd called them first thing after work.

Seven days had passed since she'd walked away from Gabe. Since she'd left her heart behind in that warm bed. The very thing she'd feared had come to pass. She'd lost him. Again. Here she was, trying to put him behind her for the second time in her life.

The difference was, she was pretty sure she loved him more now than she ever had in college. Leaving him last

Saturday morning had been the hardest moment of her life. She almost hadn't. She'd stood on his front porch for five minutes, tears dripping down her cheeks and her heart broken in little pieces, willing herself to move.

To leave him behind.

Getting over him the first time had been hard. Now? The thought of never seeing him again, never again getting to lie within his warm embrace or even to hear the addicting rumble of his laugh made her chest feel like it wanted to cave in.

Which was how she'd found herself here. Some part of her brain reminded her that this had been her choice. When she'd left, she'd been sure she'd done the right thing. She needed more than he could give her right now.

She needed him to be able to tell her he loved her, too. Now especially.

The problem was, every night since she'd left, she'd lain in bed, pondering the same awful questions. If she'd done the right thing, why did it feel like a piece of herself was missing? Was this really what she wanted? A world without him in it? She still went to bed alone. Still woke up with the same lonely ache in her chest.

She'd been right. Her time with Gabe had ruined her for any other man. She had no desire to go back to Military Match, to sit through another meaningless date. Because there was only one man she wanted. Him. And it filled her with questions she wasn't sure were smart or even logical.

Her gut twisted up in tight, confused knots, she turned sideways, glancing at the girls. "That's reckless, right? To want to see him again? Wouldn't I be settling?"

Lauren, who'd been sipping decaffeinated Earl Grey tea, looked up at her and shrugged. "But you love him, right?"

That, so far, was the easy question. She'd come to terms with it over the last seven days. "Yes. But he can't tell me he loves me, too, and he doesn't know if he'll ever get there."

One dark brow arched. "But does he make you happy?"

The weight of the world dropped onto her shoulders as the truth washed over her. She couldn't deny that, either. "Yes."

In every other way, Gabe was exactly the kind of man she'd searched her adult life for. The kind of man all little girls dream about. Honest almost to a fault. Hardworking. Dependable. A good father. And she felt whole when she was with him, like she'd found piece of herself she hadn't realized was missing.

Lauren gave her an amused smirk. "Then why are you sitting here with us?"

Steph sighed. She didn't know anymore. All she knew was that she missed him. Terribly.

Clutching her wineglass between both hands, she glanced back at Lauren. "But you didn't. You walked away from Trent for the same reason. Shouldn't I be holding out for more?"

Lauren's brow furrowed, sympathy rising in her eyes. "The difference with me and Trent is that he didn't want more. Gabe does. You said so yourself."

Mandy, seated beside Lauren on the couch, sipped at her glass of Moscato, a thoughtful expression on her face. "Seems to me that you just need to decide whether you think he's worth waiting for."

Steph's stomach rolled with nerves. She tipped her glass back and drained it. The lovely, fruity alcohol settled warm and luscious in her belly but did nothing to calm the shakiness of her limbs. "But it doesn't change anything."

The doorbell sounded through the apartment, interrupting the confusion swirling in her brain. She frowned at the girls. "Either of you expecting anybody?"

Lauren shook her head. "Not me. Trent knows where I am. If it were an emergency, he'd call me first."

Mandy shrugged. "Only person I'd be expecting is one of you, and you're already here."

Steph moved to the door, undoing the dead bolt and pulling it open... only to freeze on the spot. On the other side of the threshold, Gabe stood with his hands stuffed in his pockets. She stared for a moment, caught by the luscious sight of him. God. Of all the people to show up, it had to be him.

Gabe flashed a nervous smile, darted a glance in the direction of the living room behind her, and reached up to rub the back of his neck. "Hi. I'm sorry. It didn't occur to me you might have company. I should've known you wouldn't be alone on a Friday night."

"You're not interrupting. We were just leaving." Lauren, God bless her, glanced at the nonexistent watch on her wrist and popped off the couch like someone had stuck her in the behind with a needle. She took Mandy's wineglass from her hand, set it on the coffee table, and grabbed her arm, pulling her to her feet.

"We were?" Mandy frowned in confusion but let Lauren pull her toward the front door all the same.

"Yep. It's getting late." Tugging Mandy behind her, Lauren strode toward the coatrack, seated beside the door and snatched up their coats. "I have to get up early to make the doughnuts, and you're going to need a ride home."

Gabe turned a solemn frown on Lauren. "Please don't let me make you leave."

"You're not. I *do* have to get up early tomorrow. It's Saturday, our busiest day at the shop, and Miss Tipsy here has had a few. Can't let her drive home." Lauren gave Gabe a warm, reassuring smile, then turned to wrap an arm around Steph's shoulders. She planted a kiss to Steph's cheek, then shrugged into her coat.

"Bye, sweetie." Mandy leaned in and gave Steph a tight hug and followed Lauren out the door.

Gabe turned, his gaze on Lauren and Mandy as they moved across the landing and down the staircase. When they disappeared around the corner, he faced her again. For a moment they stood regarding each other. Tension moved like a living, breathing entity between them. Those hazel eyes searched her face as if he were waiting for something.

Then and there the decision she'd been contemplating all week made itself. She couldn't not do this. That he'd come to her just seemed like a blatant shove from the powers that be. If she didn't do this, she'd spend the next ten years lost in regret.

She drew a deep breath, but before she could summon the right words, Gabe stepped across the threshold. He stood so close his scent swirled around her, warm and masculine. "I miss you."

The words settled on her ears, their meaning like being offered a partnership. Or a lifetime supply of chocolate. Or like being told she'd won the lottery. Tears rushed up on her, the relief so profound her shoulders sagged. She'd spent the last week thinking about what she wanted from her life, from him. Had thought about her relationship with her father and all her regrets. When she'd left Gabe lying asleep in bed, she'd arrived home in tears, her chest all but splitting wide open.

She gave him the brightest smile she could muster, but her lower lip wobbled. "You came all the way over here at nine o'clock at night to tell me that?"

"Couldn't wait." He pulled a hand from his pocket and dragged it through his hair, then darted a nervous glance around him before finally settling his gaze on her again. One beefy shoulder hitched, and he let out a soft laugh. "Christ. I haven't done this in a while. All the way over here, I rehearsed everything I wanted to say to you. Now suddenly here you are and I can't remember a damn thing."

His words sent hope blossoming in her stomach like a flower in spring. Steph curled her shaking hands around her wineglass. If she didn't, she really would hurl herself at him.

She closed the door, then drew a deep breath for courage before turning and facing him again.

"Well, I'm glad you're here. You're saving me a trip." She set her wineglass on the table beside the door, where she normally left her keys, and closed that last step between them. His warm breath caressed her cheeks, sending shivers down her spine. "I've made a decision."

He shoved both hands in his pockets and gave a solemn nod. "Okay."

"I know we agreed on a fling, and we ended this because I wanted more than you could give me—" His mouth opened, but Steph shook her head and touched her index finger to his lips. "Please. Let me finish, or I'll never get it out."

Gabe closed his mouth and nodded.

She drew a deep breath and focused on his warm hazel eyes, let them give her the strength to say the words she needed him to hear. She'd given tougher suppositions in court. She could tell this man she loved him.

"I've spent the last week lying alone in bed at night, staring at my ceiling. The truth is, there's only man I want to spend my time with. I know there are things you can't give me right now, and hell." She dropped her gaze to her bare feet, staring at her bright red nail polish. She only prayed her words made sense to him. "You might not even want this, but you're here, and I have to at least say the words."

He stared at her for a long, unnerving moment, then hooked two fingers beneath her chin and tipped her gaze to his. "For the love of my sanity, Steph, say the words."

A riotous mass of butterflies did a triple looper in her stomach. Here went nothing. "I can't just let you walk out of my life again."

Gabe slid his hands into her hair, thumbs stroking her cheeks. "Say the *words*."

She rolled her eyes, because if she didn't at least try for humor, she'd cry. He was here, his gaze locked on hers. Not one man, not even Alec, had ever looked at her the way Gabe was looking at her right now. Like his life depended on every syllable she was about to utter.

That was all the confirmation she needed. She swallowed past the rising lump in her throat and set free the words she'd been holding back for too long. "I love you, and—"

Gabe covered her mouth with his, cutting off the rest of her statement. His lips all but bruised hers with the ferocity of his kiss. Steph did the only thing she could—she slid her hands up his back and lifted onto her toes to get more of him.

When he finally came up for air, they were both breathless. His chest heaved. Her heart pounded hard enough to escape through her rib cage. God, the man could kiss.

Gabe dropped his forehead to hers. "I came to a decision myself this week."

Still trying to catch her breath, she nodded, her forehead rocking against his. "And what's that?"

"I'm in love with you." He paused, as if waiting for a reaction. When she couldn't do much more than stare and process, one corner of his mouth quirked upward. "In case you missed that, I'll say it again. I'm in *love* with you."

He bent his head again, kissing her softly once, twice, then released her face and hooked her around the waist. Those big arms banded around her back, crushing her to him so hard her insane giggle came out as more of a squeak. Then he bent and buried his face in the fall of her hair. His voice came as a muffled, husky rumble from the vicinity of her neck.

"I hadn't planned on loving Julia, but I did, so her death was... hard, and I shut myself down. Oh, I got up every day. I went through the motions. Because I'm a parent with a ten-year-old daughter who needed her father to be strong." He pulled back enough to look at her, his gaze darting over her face as his hand stroked her head. "Being with you again? It's the most alive I've felt in three years. I can't let you go, either. Not being with you has been driving me crazy."

His face blurred before her as she stroked her hands over

his chest, over the warm hills and valleys of muscle. She had no idea how they'd even ended up here. It had to be a miracle for sure. Or maybe that fate Gabe had talked about a couple weeks ago. Whatever it was, she was damn grateful for it. "Come to that conclusion all by yourself, did you?"

"Not entirely." He rolled his eyes. "You have Molly to thank for some of it."

Her mind did an about-face. Steph furrowed her brow. "Molly?"

"I wanted to let you go, to let you live your life, but doing it was harder than I expected. Apparently, Molly noticed. Her husband Leo's out of town on business, so Char invited her and the girls over for dinner tonight. We were doing the dishes when she demanded to know why my face was hanging on the floor. The only thing I could tell her was I missed you. She stared at me for a minute, then laughed and punched me in the shoulder and said, 'Then what the hell are you still standing here with me for? Go get her, you fool.' I realized she was right. That I couldn't just let you go again without a fight." He hitched a shoulder, a soft flush creeping into his cheeks. "I wasn't even sure you'd want to see me."

"I wanted to see you." She slid her hands up his back, gathering him closer. Long moments passed as they stood that way, holding each other in the aftermath of what felt like a huge decision. Gabe's big hands caressed her body, sliding over her back, over the curve of her ass. Finally, unable to stand it, she laid her head on his chest. "So what now?"

His quiet laughter rumbled through his chest. "I haven't the foggiest damn idea. I hadn't really thought much beyond this point." He pulled back enough to look into her face and sipped at her mouth. His gaze followed for a moment as he tucked away a lock of her hair, his fingers gliding along the outside of her ear. "We're going to have to take this slow. I need to give Char time to adjust to your place in my life. I want to give her the space to deal with this on her terms. I won't let her be rude to you, but..."

Steph nodded, dropping her gaze to his chest. "I understand. I hated the women my father dated after Mom died. She'll need time to get to know me and learn to trust me, to learn that I don't plan to be something temporary in your lives."

"You're not, you know. It's what I decided on the way over. That I wanted you in my life however I could get you." He dropped his forehead to hers, whispering between them, "I made the mistake of letting you go once. I'm not doing it again."

"Then we'll take this one step at a time."

"One step at a time." He leaned his head beside her ear, his warm mouth closing over the sensitive lobe. "You know, I have tonight free."

A hot little shiver shot down her spine. "Does that mean you can stay?"

His tongue traveled down the side of her neck this time. "Mm-hm. Which means I have the entire night to make up for letting you leave. Do you know what I want the most?"

"What's that?" Her breathing hitched.

"I want your breasts crushed against my chest, your legs wrapped around my hips..." He closed his fingers around the globes of her ass and rocked his hips into hers. His thickening erection pushed into her lower belly, lighting that sweet fire.

"And my cock buried inside of you. This body's now mine, and I want to stake my claim on it."

She couldn't contain her quiet, half-giddy laugh. "You are such a caveman."

He chuckled and nipped at her bottom lip. "Yes, but I'm *your* caveman."

These words caught her in the chest. She reached up to stroke his stubbled cheek, her heart lighter than it had been in a while. "Yes. Yes, you are."

See the next page for a preview of
A SEAL's Honor, the next book in
JM Stewart's sexy Military Match series.

CHAPTER ONE

Of all the places he'd expected to find himself on the Fourth of July, a singles masquerade ball at the Four Seasons Hotel wasn't one of them.

Marcus Denali poked a finger into his tuxedo collar, trying to loosen the noose as he scanned the ballroom. A sea of tuxes and ball gowns spanned out in front of him, every face covered by an elaborate mask. The entire place looked like the Fourth of July section at Walmart had exploded. Red, white, and blue covered every available surface. Streamers were strung from the ceiling. U.S. flags adorned every table. Hell, they'd even scattered the floor with balloons. To top it off, a live band played on a stage on the far-right end, the music just loud enough to scrape his already shaky nerves.

Gabe, his business partner and one of his best friends, was probably laughing his ass off right about now. For the first time in months, Marcus had a date. An actual date, not his usual weekend excursion, and from a matchmaking service no less. Gabe had met his girlfriend at Military Match and had recommended the service. Gabe had gotten lucky, though; the son of a bitch had met Steph in the park for their date.

Military Match hadn't been cheap, but the woman he'd spoken with had assured him she had the highest standards for her clients. Which was the reason he'd signed up. He needed a girlfriend. Or at least someone who could play the part. A nice girl he could see for a while who'd pass Gram's muster, so she'd stop nagging him about getting married. Her complaints were always the same. He worked too much. Why wasn't he seeing anybody? When would he finally settle down? The latest argument had started because she'd called him on a Friday night and he was actually home.

Though he had to admit, he'd come tonight because he *wanted* someone to lose himself in for a while. Something a bit more than a one-night stand, but with someone who wouldn't want to tie him down.

So here he was, being strangled by a bow tie, waiting for a date he wouldn't know if she knocked him over. He'd been instructed to meet her at the entrance, but how the hell would he know her? Every woman in the room wore a mask. Was hers dark blue like his? Were the masks identical? Hell. He should've asked, but he hadn't been on an actual date in...years.

He straightened off the wall, resisting the urge to undo his tie and the top few buttons of his blasted shirt, and scanned in another direction. Five more minutes. If his date didn't show by then, he was getting the hell out of here.

A small brunette breezed through the doorway then, coming to a stop beside him. Peering into the room, she smiled but didn't look at him. "Kind of pretentious, huh?"

He ought to turn and greet her. Smile. Introduce himself. Be friendly. He couldn't muster the energy. The whole night set out before him exhausted him. The thought of the fireworks display later shattered his nerves. Since he'd retired from the marines two years ago, he'd always stayed home on the Fourth. Tonight's masquerade was barely a mile from where they'd set the damn things off.

He shrugged, aiming for friendly but aloof. "This isn't normally my kind of scene."

"I can tell. You've tugged on your collar four times in the last minute alone."

Marcus finally forced himself to glance at his companion. Her mask caught his attention. Cobalt blue, matching her eyes, with silver lace trim that ran down the right half of her face. Something about those eyes and the dark curls bouncing around her chin nagged at him as being familiar, but with the lights turned low, he couldn't see her well enough to figure out why. Was she the date he'd been waiting for?

She was gorgeous, whoever she was. The heart-shaped neckline of her black dress showed off enough cleavage to tease, filling his head with the luscious fantasy of getting to peel it off her. The sheer, wispy fabric of the skirt floated around shapely thighs he could easily envision wrapped around his hips. Someone like her was exactly what he needed. Cute but wholesome.

He straightened off the wall, tossing her a playful smile as he narrowed his gaze on her. "You've been watching me."

Amusement glinted in her eyes as she tipped her head back to look up at him. "Guilty as charged. I was told to meet

my date in this spot, and I wondered if you might be him."
She turned back to the room at large, head once again turning
as she scanned the crowd. "So, what exactly *is* your scene?"

Okay. He'd play her game. For now. He copied her stance
and turned to the watch the dancers in front of the stage.

"Somewhere quiet. To be honest, there are too many people in here for my comfort." He jabbed a finger at the flashing
ball of death in the ceiling. "And that damn disco ball is giving me a migraine. The funny part is, I used to be the party
guy."

At least, he had been before his sister, Ava, died. And
before his time in Afghanistan. Things like binge drinking
gained a whole other appeal when you'd watched good men
get ripped apart by an IED. When you had to watch friends
die. He couldn't forget, either, sitting in that damn hospital,
staring at Ava's lifeless body, praying somehow she'd wake up.

His date stood quiet a moment. "When'd you get out?"

The soft tone of her voice told him she understood, and
relief relaxed the tight knot in his gut. This was the main
reason he'd opted to go with Military Match. So he wouldn't
have to explain to yet another woman why a small dive bar
was ten times more comfortable than the thought of going
into a crowded nightclub. Or why loud music was akin to
sandpaper to his nerves, rubbing them raw.

"Retired two years ago." He darted a sidelong glance at
her. "Why Military Match? Did you serve?"

As she looked over at him, her chin lifted and pride filled
her eyes. "No. My father and my brother did. Marines."

"Ooh-rah." He grinned, straightened off the wall, and
turned fully to face her. "Inquiring minds want to know. Who

were you told to meet?"

"Tall, dark, and handsome and..." A slow, cheeky grin spread across her face as she tugged the corner of his tie. "Wearing a blue bow tie."

"In that case, looks like I'm your man." He winked and gave her a two-fingered salute, then stuck out his hand. "I'm—"

She pressed a finger to his lips, halting the word before he could tell her his name, and shook her head.

"No names yet. Part of the fun of this ball is the anonymity the masks give us, right? I could be anybody. So, pretend I'm your dream girl and dance with me." She didn't give him time to approve or deny the request, but winked and grabbed his hand, tugging him behind her. At the edge of the crowd in front of the stage, she turned to him. "This is a salsa. Do you know how?"

His grandmother had spent hours teaching him and Ava to dance. He knew the salsa...along with the mambo, the waltz, *and* the foxtrot. Not something he'd normally brag about, but the knowledge came in handy every once in a while. Like now.

He listened for a moment, then stepped into the beat, added a few flourishes, including a turn, then winked and held out his hand. "The question is, do you?"

"Impressive." Her grin widening, she took his hand, stepping into the dance with him.

The quick tempo meant he had to concentrate on his steps, on her movements, so that the crowd around him, the music, ceased to exist. There were only those flirty blue eyes and the sway of her hips. He had to hand it to her. She wasn't a beginner by any stretch of the imagination. Her movements weren't stiff, like she followed some remembered set of steps, but fluid, her hips swaying to the natural rhythm of the music like she'd done it her whole life.

The sway of those hips filled his head with more fantasies. What expression would cross those features when her orgasm took hold of her? He had the sudden, overwhelming desire to watch the heat flare in her eyes as her body rose to his...

The song ended far too soon, the tempo slowing to the steady pulse of a heartbeat. The couples around them all shifted, tugging each other closer. Marcus and his mysterious companion stopped moving. She stared up at him, eyes soft, chest heaving with her breathlessness. The need to feel her body against his hit him hard. It had been too damn long since he'd last indulged in the pleasures of the flesh in the feminine form.

Unable to resist, he lifted a brow. When in Rome... "Care for another dance?"

She smiled, nodded, and he tugged her close, settling one hand against her lower back. They swayed to the soft strains of the music in silence, movements stiff and awkward, but those blue eyes never left his. Despite the crowd and the over-whelming buzz in his head, the knot that had formed in his gut when he arrived finally loosened.

He released her hand, wrapped both arms around her in-stead, and pulled her closer. Her small, curvy body swayed against him, her soft belly brushing his with every subtle movement. So close he could feel the hammering of her heart against his chest.

He ducked down, leaning his cheek against the top of her

head so she'd hear him over the music. "If you won't tell me your name, at least give me something. What's a nice girl like you doing in a place like this?"

She let out a quiet laugh and leaned back enough to peer at him. "I wanted a nice guy. This place has an excellent reputation for the kind of people they accept."

Also why he'd used the service. Not that he'd tell her that. No, he wanted to hear that addicting laugh again. So he tossed her a smile. "How do you know I'm one of the nice guys?"

"Because you served. I've found enough playboys to be able to recognize the good guys when I see them. And most guys who served are the good ones." She averted her gaze to the right, something somber moving over her. One corner of her mouth hitched upward. "Just do me a favor, huh? Don't tell me I remind you of your sister. At least not yet. Give me a running start first."

Despite the voice in his head telling him not to say the words, he couldn't resist leaning his mouth beside her ear. "Trust me, angel. What I'm thinking right now has very little to do with my sister."

A tremor moved through her he felt clean down to his fucking toes and set his libido thrumming. Marcus stifled a groan. Five minutes with her and already she had his cock swelling against his fly.

It didn't help that when she met his gaze again, those blue eyes filled with an intoxicating combination of heat and challenge. "What *are* you thinking?"

He really shouldn't toy with her, but this was the most fun he'd had in…hell, he couldn't remember. "Oh, I definitely can't tell you that. I'm supposed to be playing the gentleman tonight, remember?"

The heaviness hanging over her finally lifted. She let out a quiet laugh. "Well, at least you're honest."

Triumph surged in his chest. It would probably get into him trouble at some point, but he had a feeling he'd make an ass out of himself in order to hear that laugh again. It ought to scare the hell out of him. He'd spent his life determined to keep people at a distance. You couldn't get hurt if you didn't expect anybody to actually stick around. Something about her, though, relaxed his nerves.

He shook his head and chuckled. "Suddenly I'm not sorry I put on this damn monkey suit."

"Me either." She averted her gaze off to her right again, but this time her smile was genuine. "You look pretty hot in that tux."

He ducked his head, leaning his mouth beside her ear again. It was pushing his luck to say this, but hell, he was going for broke. Just to hear her laugh again would be reward enough. "You're inspiring some very naughty thoughts yourself in that dress."

"Oh, now you're just laying it on thick." Her eyes glinted with playful impishness as she arched a brow. "You didn't actually think it would get you anywhere, did you?"

He let out a dramatic sigh. "A guy can hope."

She laughed again, light and airy, and damned if he could stop from smiling along with her. They spent the rest of the song in silence, somewhere between oddly comfortable and a fine sweet tension that arced between them. It was subtle. More in the shift of her body. She leaned into him and rested her forehead against his chin. He was hard as steel, but if she noticed she didn't say anything or even push away.

"Tell me your name, angel." He wanted to roll it around on his tongue and taste the flavor of it. She intrigued the hell out of him, and he wanted more. A feeling he hadn't had in...shit. Practically forever. Most of the women he dated were temporary, women who didn't want to be tied down any more than he did.

For tonight he gave himself permission to go with it. Tonight was the anniversary of Ava's death. Finding a weekend hookup had long since lost its appeal, but tonight he needed the company or he'd drive himself insane.

Instead of the quiet murmur he'd expected, his companion stopped moving. She stood so still the back of his neck prickled, heat moving over the surface of his skin. Her awareness of him sparked in the air like a living, breathing entity.

He pulled back and winked at her in a vain attempt to set her at ease. "I have to know whose name I'm going to be calling out later."

If she slapped him for that, he'd deserve it, but he *hoped* she'd laugh and then finally relax. When she didn't, when she leaned back instead, her eyes studying his face as if searching for the clues to life, his gut knotted.

He shrugged. "Sorry. Bad joke. You were supposed to call me out for being cocky, tell me how full of myself I am..."

Nothing.

He let out an uncomfortable laugh and stroked her back. "Angel, if you don't say something I'm just going to keep babbling. Do me a favor and save me from myself, huh?"

Finally, she drew her shoulders back. "Mandy."

The name rolled around in his brain. Lodged there. Another small brunette inserted herself into his thoughts. With similar blue eyes, big and wide in her face, and the softest mouth this side of the Mississippi. He studied his companion's face. The similarities were there, but surely she couldn't be *that* Mandy.

His heart now hammering from the vicinity of his throat, he drew a deep breath and forced a calm that came from experience. He was a marine, damn it. One little brunette would not throw him off his game.

He smiled and prayed she didn't notice the way his hands shook. "Mandy's a very pretty name. Got a last name to go with that?"

Again she stared. Her throat bobbed. Her mask trembled as she reached up and pulled it off, revealing her full face.

His heart stuttered to a stop. Son of a *bitch*. So that's why she'd looked familiar—he'd been seeing her in his dreams.

Of all the women in Seattle, they'd fixed him up with the one woman he wanted more than he wanted to breathe... and the only woman he couldn't touch with a ten-foot pole: his buddy's kid sister.

About the Author

JM Stewart is a coffee and chocolate addict who lives in the Pacific Northwest with her husband, two sons, and two very spoiled dogs. She's a hopeless romantic who believes everybody should have their happily ever after and has been devouring romance novels for as long as she can remember. Writing them has become her obsession.

Learn more at:

AuthorJMStewart.com

Facebook.com/AuthorJMStewart

Twitter: @JMStewartWriter

www.ingramcontent.com/pod-product-compliance
Ingram Content Group UK Ltd.
Pitfield, Milton Keynes, MK11 3LW, UK
UKHW021150020325
455674UK00006B/43

9 781538 728857